THE HUMMINGBIRD HOUSE PRESENTS

Love, From The Hummingbird House

And

The Easter Charade

Two Hummingbird House Novellas

By Donna Ball

www.donnaball.net

Published by Blue Merle Publishing
Drawer H
Mountain City, Georgia 30562

www.bluemerlepublishers.com

*This is a work of fiction. All places, characters,
events and organizations mentioned in this book are
either the product of the author's imagination or
used fictitiously.*

Cover Art **www.bigstock.com**

ISBN: 978-1-7351271-0-1

First printing May 2020

Love, From The Hummingbird House

Or
Never Judge a Book by Its Cover

If this is your first visit to the Hummingbird House, here's a little background:

Best friends and empty-nesters Bridget, Cici and Lindsay gave up their suburban Baltimore lifestyle to restore a 100-year-old mansion in the heart of the Shenandoah Valley (*A YEAR ON LADYBUG FARM*). Inspired by the bucolic life their friends made for themselves in the country, Paul Slater, a renowned author and style expert, and his partner Derrick Anderson, owner of a highly successful Washington art gallery, left it all behind to purchase a rambling old lodge with multicolored doors a few miles away from their friends on Ladybug Farm (*VINTAGE LADYBUG FARM*). They were quickly joined by the flamboyant and eccentric Harmony Haven, who came for a weekend and took up permanent residence, and by Purline Williams, a twenty-something local girl, who took over the kitchen, the housekeeping, and her employers with an efficiency matched only by her bullheadedness. Though Paul and Derrick could not have been more unsuited both for country life and the hospitality industry, their natural compassion and instinctive gift for entertaining—along with a generous dose of help from their friends—soon made The Hummingbird House Bed and Breakfast a destination of distinction. (*THE HUMMINGBIRD HOUSE*). Those who visit there may not always find what they expect, but they always find what they need.

And now you're all caught up. Enjoy your visit to The Hummingbird House, and come again soon!

~*~

From *The Happy Traveler* blog
February 13

Nestled in a cozy woodland in the heart of the Shenandoah Valley, the unsuspecting traveler will be delightfully surprised by the quaint eclecticism of The Hummingbird House Bed and Breakfast. It's a charming lodge-style dwelling surrounded by park-like gardens—which one can imagine to be utterly enchanting in full bloom-- and water features which, I'm assured, provide a soothing musical backdrop for evening strolls in warmer weather. And while the majestic snow-capped mountains against which the lodge is set don't actually provide any ski slopes (one can only imagine how exciting it would be if they did!) they are nonetheless quite picturesque to look at.

While some might think that February is a dismal time to visit the Virginia heartland, long-time readers of this page will recall the number one rule of the Happy Traveler: Be prepared for something wonderful! Proprietors Paul Slater and Derrick Anderson promise an elegant Valentine's weekend filled with champagne, chocolate and romance—even for a single lady like me! Yes, it's a Fairy Tale Booklover's Valentine Day Gala, and guess what? It even includes a visit by royalty! Well, more or less...

~*~

~1~

"I *told* you it would be a success." Derrick practically chortled as he peeked into the reception parlor where a half dozen guests laughed and chatted before the fire, glasses of rich red merlot in hand. "You said no one wants to spend Valentine's Day way out here in the middle of nowhere with not even a ski slope around when the Virginia countryside is practically *riddled* with romantic B&Bs that cater to lovers, and I said why do we have to make Valentine's Day about lovers? Why can't we make it about *book* lovers? And you said…"

Paul winced. "I know what I said."

"And then I said, the key is romance! Specifically, the *queen* of romance," concluded Derrick triumphantly. "And I still say if we had announced she was coming we could have had twice as many reservations."

"We couldn't possibly have had twice as many. We're booked up." Paul pretended to be put-upon as he fussed with the lavish bouquet of roses on the reception desk, although his self-satisfaction was difficult to hide. "You do know that Valentine's Day was invented by florists solely for the purpose of price-gouging a product that no one would otherwise buy in the dead of winter, don't you?"

"Everyone knows that." Derrick gave a dismissive wave of his hand. "All I'm saying is that if we'd announced that we'd snagged Esmerelda Delaware— the aforementioned Queen of Romance—as our guest speaker we could have booked the entire house *without* the book club reunion—and they got a discount, you know! And that's not even to mention the prince! Why—"

"Oh, please!" Their friend Cici came up behind them, her blue eyes sparkling. "It's not like you're giving Lindsay, Bridget and me free rooms, you know. We live just down the road. Kiki and Ted are the only book club people who got a discount and you know they're going to be the life of the party. Gosh, it will be good to see them again! Don't you just love reunions?"

"Adore them," Paul agreed, turning from the roses to brush her cheek with a kiss. "Everyone is always fat and bald—except us, of course. When did you get here, darling? Where are the girls?"

"Bridget's helping Purline with the hors d'oeuvres and Harmony cornered Lindsay in the hall. Harmony's telling her fortune, I think. Wait." She blinked and stared at Paul, her eyes wide. "Did you say prince? What prince?"

Derrick stifled a groan. "I asked Harmony not to bother our guests with that nonsense this weekend."

Paul answered Cici's question. "Darling, didn't you hear? Esmerelda Delaware married herself a prince. Some little country in the Baltic states I think. She takes him everywhere with her, on tour, to reader's conventions, on talk shows…"

"I hear he's absolutely *adorbs*," Derrick confided. "Half her age, of course—"

"Or a quarter," put in Paul. And he added gently to his partner, "No one says 'adorbs' anymore, darling."

Derrick went on, not in the least offended, "With one of those luscious accents and some kind of military uniform…"

"And a sword," Paul added, arching one eyebrow just slightly.

Cici grinned and glanced around. "Are they here?"

"They're due any minute," Paul said.

"But Kiki got here an hour ago," Derrick said. "She's in the yellow room."

"Canary," corrected Paul.

"And we have a perfectly darling couple of ladies from Maine down for the weekend. Huge fans of Miss Delaware's," Derrick went on. "They're in the purple room."

Paul rolled his eyes with an air of long-suffering. "Lilac," he said. "The *lilac* room."

"And next to them is a couple from Tennessee celebrating the anniversary of their first date. He says he's never heard of Miss Delaware but *she* says *Love's First Kiss* is the reason she agreed to go out with him in the first place. But she promises he won't interfere with the book discussion," Derrick concluded. "He's just here for the free champagne."

"Well, it *is* Valentine's Day," Cici reminded him.

"A completely manufactured holiday," Paul began.

"Just so that florists can charge more for roses," Cici finished for him, "I know. What about Ted?" She looked around again. "He's coming, isn't he? It wouldn't be a party without Ted."

"He's due to check in by four," Paul said. "Red room." He scowled in annoyance. "I mean rose. *Rose* room."

"You probably heard that tech company he bought into paid off in a big way a few years back," Derrick said, "and he took early retirement from the accounting firm to sow some wild oats as the world's most eligible bachelor. But the big news is," Derrick finished, his eyes gleaming suggestively, "he is *not* bringing a companion this weekend."

Cici's eyebrows went up. "He's single? Now that is a surprise. I've never known Ted to be without a girlfriend for longer than it took to change his sheets."

"If he had been," declared Bridget as she came in from the kitchen, "one of the girls in book club would have snatched him up before his head could stop spinning. Everything looks gorgeous, boys!" She hugged Paul, and then Derrick. "Thanks for letting us crash the party. I brought chocolate-chocolate cake and red velvet cookies."

"Of course you did, you dear thing!" Paul kissed both her cheeks. "How could we *not* invite you?"

"The point is," Derrick said, a trifle impatiently, "Ted is single, Kiki's single…"

Bridget said, "Really? When did that happen?"

"Divorced," explained Derrick, "two years ago. And she always had *such* a mad crush on Ted. So…"

"Seriously, do you think so?" Cici frowned a little. "I know they've always been thick as thieves—they've known each other since grammar school, after all—but I never saw it as a romantic thing."

"Really, Cici, you were completely clueless about what was going on around you back then," Paul said. "Why, you were the only one in book club who actually read the book—every month!"

"I read the book," Bridget objected. Then she admitted, "Most of the time."

"The point is," Derrick put in firmly, "I have it on good authority that the two of them have kept in touch over the years, and have been texting back and forth quite a lot the past few months, and the buzz is…"

"Oh, sweetie." Paul winced, sighing. "No one says 'buzz' anymore."

"The buzz," Derrick repeated deliberately, "is that this might be a reunion in more ways than one. Something special is definitely in the air."

Bridget looked skeptical. "I don't know, Derrick. I mean, I love Ted and all, and he's a ton of fun—I mean, could anyone even *think* of giving a party without him?"

"He has this way of putting everyone at ease," Cici agreed. "And he always sees the best in every situation. He's positively the most upbeat person I've ever known."

"Exactly," said Bridget with a nod. "But it's almost as though—and don't misunderstand me because I do adore him—but as though all that happiness was hiding something a little sad. I just always thought there was something, I don't know, off about him."

"As in, in-the-closet off?" suggested Cici.

"Oh, please!" Paul scoffed. "Just because a man likes Yanni doesn't mean he's gay." He thought about that for a minute and added, "Merely that he has bad taste."

"Don't listen to him," Derrick said. "His gay-dar is worse than yours. He didn't even know *I* was gay until we'd been dating three months."

"I didn't mean gay," Bridget said before Paul could reply. "I just meant all that sleeping around always seemed a little desperate to me. As though he was looking for something he could never find. It always worried me."

"Unless," Derrick said, his expression brightening, "what he was looking for was Kiki! She's held up really well, by the way, except for one, well, rather dubious hair color choice. I don't think he'll be disappointed."

"Now, now, now," Paul chided in a bored tone, "let's try to avoid the incredibly obvious clichés, shall we, and stick with the merely obvious ones? We already have a romance writer married to a dashing prince half her age—"

"A quarter," Derrick supplied.

Paul nodded approval, continuing, "Cherubs dancing from every possible corner, cocktail napkins shaped like little hearts and enough roses to fill a funeral parlor. Must we have the whole star-crossed-lovers-united-at-last drama as well? I'm half-inclined to call the Hallmark Channel."

Cici grinned and Derrick slipped his arm affectionately through Paul's. "He's really a hopeless romantic, you know."

Cici said, "Well, I think it sounds like a fabulous weekend that would be even more fabulous with a glass of wine. So if you'll excuse me…"

"Gentlemen," announced a sonorous voice behind them, "we're in agreement. There's no point in postponing the bad news."

They turned to see Harmony, the B &B's general manager and resident mystic, sail through the antique French doors that opened from the foyer, the great prow of her bosom leading the way, a flutter of purple and red silk caftan flowing behind. Lindsay trailed in her wake, looking bemused.

Harmony placed a sheet of paper filled with arcane symbols on the reception desk with a flourish, smoothed out the wrinkles, and regarded it with a sort of grim satisfaction. Lindsay put forth timidly, "Actually, I didn't agree to anything."

Harmony ignored her. "There's no point in denying what's written in the stars," she announced.

"This entire event is doomed. The only way to salvage your business is to cancel the weekend."

~*~

From *The Happy Traveler* Blog

Of course an essential part of any B&B experience is the personality your hosts bring to the ambience. While Mr. Slater and Mr. Anderson are clearly gentlemen of great distinction and impeccable taste whose only concern would appear to be to anticipate the needs of each and every guest, I must confess the piece de resistance *for me was the delightfully eccentric Miss Harmony Haven. She does triple duty on staff as the Hummingbird House general manager, massage therapist, and fortune teller. Do not on any account miss her hot stone massage, and if you can possibly persuade her to read your palm do, dear readers, I beg you, do. Not only are her readings enlightening and compassionate—rather like an hour spent with a good shrink, only at half the price!—her predictions are often uncannily accurate…*

~*~

~2~

"It really is clear for anyone to see," Harmony said, brandishing her multi-ringed fingers over the bizarre-looking sketch she had spread out on the desk. "Pluto is in Scorpio, the sign of sex, square Venus, the sign of love and friendship, in the house of secrets and deception, not to mention Mercury being retrograde in the house of communication...boys, it is nothing short of a Valentine's Day disaster waiting to happen!"

Paul regarded her politely. "Perhaps if we hung a pentagram above the door," he suggested.

Derrick looked slightly more concerned. "What is this?" He pointed to a symbol surrounded by squiggly lines at the bottom of what they all by now had realized was an astrological chart.

"Only a total eclipse of the moon," she pronounced triumphantly, "on Valentine's Day no less! And it couldn't be in a less propitious spot for celebrations and reunions."

"Huh," said Bridget, musing. "I don't think I knew the moon had eclipses. You learn something new every day."

Cici asked curiously, "So why didn't you mention all this before? I mean, it does seem a little last-minute for a disaster-waiting-to-happen."

Harmony rolled her eyes expressively toward Paul. "As though I haven't been trying for the last month! The signs couldn't have been more clear."

Paul gave her a dismissive pat on the shoulder. "Not that I'm not grateful for your concern, darling, but the only sign I'm interested in is the dollar sign. Hopefully in multiples."

And Derrick added uneasily, "It really is too late to do anything about it now."

"All I'm saying," insisted Harmony firmly, "is that the best of intentions can sometimes do more harm than good. And with the Happy Traveler due to post a review any time now we *really* can't afford any mistakes."

"Who's the Happy Traveler?" Lindsay wanted to know.

Again Paul was dismissive. "Just some blogger."

"She has 600,000 followers on Twitter!" Harmony replied indignantly. "It's a huge coup to even get a mention on her blog."

"The thing is," Derrick explained, "she always books her stays anonymously, so you never know when she's coming—or who she is when she gets here."

Bridget nodded. "Like one of those fancy food critics."

"Well, if a food critic is *really* fancy, everyone knows who he is," Lindsay pointed out. "With The Food Network and all."

"At any rate," Paul said, "the one thing we know for certain is that the Happy Traveler, whoever she is, won't be here this weekend." And he lifted a meaningful eyebrow. "Unless it's one of you girls. Everyone else checks out."

The ladies grinned and Paul's gaze suddenly went over their shoulder. "Purline!" he called, moving forward toward the jeaned and pony-tailed young woman with the tray in her hands who was striding purposefully toward the parlor. "Purline, I told you, the hot canapés don't come out until 5:00! Five darling, five-oh." He took the tray from her. "The cheese platter first, my dear, remember?"

Purline snapped her gum at him. "Them sausage rolls is going to be mush by 5:00."

"They're not sausage rolls," Paul replied, looking insulted. He turned back toward the kitchen with the tray. "They're ground artisanal pork organically seasoned with locally sourced spices and wrapped in puff pastry."

"They're sausage rolls," confided Bridget as Paul shouldered his way through the swinging doors to the kitchen. "I made them myself."

Purline stopped to glance at the papers spread out on the reception desk on her way to the kitchen. She looked barely old enough to be out of high school, but she ran the daily operations of the Hummingbird House with all the efficiency of a military barracks. "That queen called," she told Derrick, "while you-all was busy pouring wine for everybody. Or at least her secretary did. Said something about snow in New York." Purline tilted one of the papers toward her with her fingertip. "What in the world is this hen-scratching?"

Derrick stared at her blankly for a moment and then his face cleared. "Oh! You mean Ms. Delaware." Then his expression turned to alarm. "Wait. Snow in New York? Is her flight cancelled? What did she say? I'd better call back." He hurried toward the office at the back of the house.

Purline frowned over the paper and then looked at Harmony accusingly. "Is this more of that voodoo you've been spouting all over the house the past month?" She rolled her eyes and resumed her course to the kitchen. "Lord Jesus, take me now and deliver me from this den of iniquity."

Harmony followed Derrick's retreating back with a glum expression as she gathered the astrological charts close to her chest. "Disaster," she intoned.

"Cici! Bridget! Lindsay! Can it be? Is that really you?"

The three women turned to see a tall, well kept woman in a pink-streaked bob crossing the foyer toward them, hands extended. They rushed to greet her with squeals of delight. "Kiki!"

~3~

The seven-member book club had begun in the 1990s when Cici, Bridget, Lindsay, Paul and Derrick all lived in the Baltimore suburbs, and it had thrived for over a decade. They took turns meeting at each other's houses over coffee and cake or wine and cheese— mostly wine—and even took to the road when the occasion demanded—a Savannah, Georgia B&B for *Midnight in the Garden of Good and Evil,* for example, and a week in a Dublin farmhouse when they read *Angela's Ashes.* Inevitably, they all became close friends, and just as inevitably, some were closer than others.

It took the women less than fifteen minutes to cover the usual "What have you been up to?" and "Did you hear about…" , mostly because Cici, Bridget and Lindsay could tell that Kiki was practically bursting with news, and because they were dying to hear it.

"So," Lindsay prompted impatiently, having waited long enough, "What's this I hear about you and Ted? Anything you want to share?"

Kiki pressed her fingers against her lips in an imitation of surprise, her eyes dancing. "What on earth are you talking about? Who's been gossiping?"

"Who do you think?" Cici replied impatiently. "We don't need the internet around here for news, as long as we have Derrick. So what's the scoop?"

Lindsay, Cici, Bridget and Kiki were settled in the reception parlor on the velvet sofa adjacent to the fireplace, wine glasses in hand, leaning in close as they waited for Kiki to share her confidences. Other groups had formed around the room in the usual cocktail hour conversation, but none held quite the intensity of theirs.

"Well…" Kiki said, clearly enjoying herself as she drew out the suspense. "I don't want to let the cat out of the bag, but it could be pretty big news."

Bridget's eyes widened with anticipation. "Really? Tell!"

Kiki glanced around, as though to ensure she would not be overheard, and leaned in a little closer. "I don't think anyone else knows this, but when we were younger, before I married Phil of course, Ted and I had a little fling."

The other women pretended to be surprised, although no one really was. Ted had that kind of reputation, after all.

"It didn't last long, and we both decided we were *much* better off as friends," Kiki went on, "but we made one of those promises, like people do—if we were both still single when we were fifty, we'd marry each other. Then, of course, I got married, and the years went by, and we got comfortable being best friends. When I moved to Denver…"

"Oh," said Cici, "I didn't know that!"

She nodded. "Phil's company transferred him. It was a big promotion, so naturally we took it. Then, just as we were getting settled, they offered him another promotion—in Canada. And he decided to take it without me."

The other women winced, and Kiki tossed back a gulp of wine. "He said he wasn't sure he wanted to be married anymore. Not sure! His exact words." She shrugged. "I kept the house, of course."

"And you came all the way back here for this weekend?" Lindsay said.

"Of course I did!" Kiki's eyes sparkled. "And if things work out the way I think they will, I might just be staying. Ted was *so* excited when he heard about this reunion—and on Valentine's Day of all things!—how could I *not* come? He said, and I quote, 'This will be the beginning of a whole new chapter for us.' A whole new chapter!"

She took another quick sip of wine. "But I'm getting ahead of myself. I guess you heard Ted made a lot of money on that A.I. company he invested in—this wasn't long after the book club broke up—and he was going through one of those midlife crisis things, talking about feeling like he'd been living someone else's life, needing to make a major change, that kind of thing. I guess I kind of helped him through it, because the next thing I know he's decided to move to Europe and is giving me the credit for changing his life. Of course, I was in the middle of moving across country myself then, so he wasn't the only one whose life was changing. We texted and e-mailed back and forth, then fell out of touch for awhile—my fault, mostly," she added with a self-deprecating grimace, "since I was a little distracted by the fact that my marriage was falling apart. Then, after the divorce..."

"I'm so sorry," Bridget said kindly, covering Kiki's hand briefly with hers. The other women murmured agreement.

"Oh, it was the best thing," Kiki assured them fervently. "The *best* thing. No regrets at all. Because when I changed my status on Facebook last year Ted reached out again to offer sympathy, you know, and we started texting back and forth again. Only this time it was different. *He* was different. Calmer, maybe. More confident. He said he'd finally found himself, and that I'd given him the courage to do it. We were texting ten or twelve times a day, talking about things we'd never talked about before. Important things. Real things." She hesitated, her expression thoughtful. "I started to realize that I'd never really known him before, and that was probably why things hadn't worked out between us the first time. And then…" Her eyes lit up. "It turns out he felt the same way! He said I changed his life. He said I might even have saved it. All those other women…he said they were all just foils for his true feelings, and that I was the only woman he could ever really be himself with, the one who taught him how to love."

"Well," said Bridget, raising her eyebrows to hear her own theory confirmed—in part, at least. Lindsay and Cici exchanged looks that weren't particularly surprised.

"*And…*" Kiki drew in a breath and paused for dramatic effect. "Remember that promise we made? The one about marrying each other if we're still single at age 50? Well, I mentioned something it about it a month or so ago, and he texted back, 'We should definitely talk about that'—so he's been thinking about it too. And right after that he told me about this book lovers weekend and insisted I meet him here. Insisted! He said this Valentine's Day would be the one that we'd both remember forever. He said it would be the first day of the rest of our lives."

Lindsay raised an eyebrow. "Wow, it does sound serious. Very romantic! I always did think you and Ted were awfully cute together."

"But," Cici pointed out, "you haven't seen him in what? Five years? A lot can change in that amount of time."

"A lot *has* changed," Kiki agreed. "That's the whole point. Everything has changed. This might finally be our happily-ever-after."

Lindsay added, "As long as he hasn't gotten fat or bald or anything."

Kiki laughed giddily, waving the idea away. "I wouldn't care if he had!"

"But he hasn't, has he?" Bridget pressed. "Because he was such a good-looking man! I would've killed for his cheekbones. Not to mention his eyelashes."

Kiki shrugged. "I don't know. He's not much of one for sending photos. And all men have eyelashes to die for. It's one of God's little jokes."

Cici lifted a skeptical eyebrow. "Well, I for one wouldn't move all the way across the country just for a man, I don't care how long his eyelashes are. Maybe see how the weekend goes first?"

Kiki beamed. "Oh, I don't think it's going to take the whole weekend. Tomorrow is Valentine's Day, after all. And girls, if he doesn't beat me to it, I think…." She pressed both hands over her heart, her color rising. "I think I'm going to propose!"

~*~

From *The Happy Traveler* blog

Upon first approach to the Hummingbird House, one can't help being struck by the almost dizzying array of doors—each one painted a different bright, glossy color and each one opening onto a deep rocking-chair porch that wraps completely around the lodge. Thank heavens our gracious hosts have marked the entrance clearly with a "Welcome" sign! But even if they hadn't, it would be difficult to get lost because upon making a reservation each guest is assigned a color: You, dear, will be in the rose room, and you in the lilac, and you in the canary. The rooms are tastefully accessorized in colors that match the door, down to the towels and the fresh-flower bouquets! Charming, am I right?

A downy king-sized bed awaits the weary traveler, complete with brushed Egyptian cotton sheets and pillows dressed in eyelet and lace. A carafe of sherry and two crystal glasses were waiting on my dresser, along with a Godiva chocolate on the pillow. Each bath is unique of course, but mine has a lovely claw foot tub and a canister of absolutely heavenly-smelling rose bath crystals.

And speaking of heavenly, cocktail hour is definitely not to be missed! An array of imported cheeses greeted us, along with glasses of a very nice local merlot. Later came the hot hors d'ouvres—sausage wraps with a piquant dipping sauce, stuffed mushrooms, warm brie with freshly baked French bread—it almost makes dinner redundant, particularly for those of us watching our figures (not to mention our cholesterol!) But how foolish would you be to turn down one of the Hummingbird House's delectable food-and-wine pairing dinners, which have become famous all over this part of the state? On special occasions, like this Valentine's Day Book Lover's Gala, I'm delighted to say, dinner is included in the weekend package—a real treat for those of us who have reached an age where we don't like to go exploring strange countryside after dark in search of sustenance. The menu, which I found printed in scrolled font on ivory parchment paper propped up on my pillow, sounds quite sophisticated for a country inn, and if the aromas wafting from the kitchen are any indication, the feast that awaits us will be...well, heavenly.

~*~

~4~

"Crisis averted!" declared Derrick, pressing a hand over his heart as he hurried back to the reception desk. "Ms. Delaware's flight was canceled out of New York but they were able to drive to Philadelphia and get the train to Washington, where they were able to find a car and driver. They're driving in tonight and should be here for dinner, as planned.

"That's an awful lot of bustling for a woman of her age." Paul looked vaguely distracted as he checked the reservation page on the computer.

"I don't know why you say that," Derrick objected. "You have no idea how old she is."

"Oh please. She had to be sixty the last time she had her book jacket photo retouched... and that was twenty years ago."

Derrick started to reply but was interrupted by Cici, who came from the parlor followed closely by Bridget. "Is it okay if we pour a couple of glasses of champagne early?" Cici asked, her eyes sparkling with a secretive amusement. "And you have *got* to come join us. Kiki has some very, well, interesting news."

Derrick was quick to agree. "Sure sweetie, help yourself to one of the bottles leftover from the brunch mimosas. One that's already open, of course, you don't want to take the fizz out of the good stuff. What news? Is it a secret? I'm right behind you."

Bridget said, "I'm bringing out the cheese tray. Weren't there strawberries on it? We definitely need strawberries."

"What news?" Derrick repeated eagerly, starting to follow them to the kitchen. "Just a hint?"

But he turned back at the opening of the front door, and the women moved toward the kitchen without him. A burst of cold February air accompanied the entrance of a slender, elegant redhead in a belted camel coat and stiletto heeled velvet boots. She stood for a moment, smiling as she took in the ambience, and then started toward the desk.

"Who is that?" Derrick's voice dropped to a whisper as he edged back behind the desk and bent down to look over Paul's shoulder. "Isn't everyone already here?"

"That's what I'm trying to figure out," Paul returned sotto voce. He clicked the mouse and another screen appeared. "I saw her drive up. You don't suppose she got her reservation date confused, do you?"

"But we're completely booked up!" Panic danced in Derrick's eyes and his whisper went shrill. "This weekend of all weekends, what can we possibly do with a walk-in guest?" Then, without missing a beat, he spun to face the desk with a warm smile on his face and greeted the new arrival. "Good afternoon and welcome to the Hummingbird House! Do you happen to have a reservation?"

She was in her late forties—or early fifties, presupposing an excellent plastic surgeon-- with high cheekbones and expertly applied makeup. Her shoulder length auburn hair was feathered with flattering gold highlights, and her green eyes sparkled in a way that completely belied her age as she swept the room once more with her gaze. "What an absolutely enchanting place!" she declared in a warm and vibrant contralto. "More than I ever imagined! You two really do have the magic touch, don't you?"

Paul stood, trying to hide his confusion behind a polite smile. "Thank you for saying so. But I'm terribly sorry to tell you we're all booked up this weekend."

"Oh, I have a reservation," she assured him gaily. "It's under Ted Butler."

Paul and Derrick exchanged a look, and then Derrick said quickly, "Oh! Oh, of course. It's just that we were given to understand Ted would be coming alone this weekend. Not a problem, of course…"

"Unless you're Kiki," Paul muttered in Derrick's ear, but kept his smile in place.

"… your room has a lovely king-sized bed," Derrick went on, unfazed, "and I'll send the housekeeper around with more towels as soon as we get you settled. Is Ted bringing the rest of your luggage? I'll just go unlock the door so he can take it directly inside from the porch."

Derrick started around the desk but she said, "No need." She gestured toward the suede overnight bag at her feet. "This is all I have. I can manage."

"I beg your pardon," Paul said, peering at her hesitantly, "but have we met? Or perhaps I've seen your photograph. You look terribly familiar."

She chuckled softly. "Honestly, Paul, you always were a shameless flirt. Of course we've met."

Derrick looked at Paul curiously, and Paul gave a small shake of his head. "I'm sorry, I don't…"

"Look closer," she insisted, amused.

He did, and some of the color left his face. He clutched Derrick's arm, and Derrick looked at the stranger more intently. His jaw went slack. The two men looked at each other, and then Derrick took a step back, gripping the desk, seeming momentarily robbed of speech. It was Paul who said, his voice cracking with incredulity, "*Ted?*"

~5~

Behind them, there was a crash as Cici lost her grip on the four freshly filled wine glasses she had been balancing in her two hands. The cheese tray rattled in Bridget's hands and a couple of ripe strawberries rolled to the floor. Both women stared at the newcomer. Harmony, pausing on the way to the dining porch to check the seating arrangement, watched with interest.

"It is," whispered Bridget with lips that barely moved. "It *is* him."

"Her," corrected Cici, unblinking. "*Her.*"

At the sound of the broken glasses the three people at the desk had turned toward them, and now the woman exclaimed in delight, "Cici? Bridget? Oh my God, you look fabulous!" She rushed forward to embrace them each in turn. "How is it possible that you never change?"

Bridget stood like a statue as the other woman hugged her, her eyes big, her voice small. "I guess we can't say the same about you."

She laughed, tossing back her luxurious mane of auburn hair, and held out her arms as she did a little spin. "Do you like it? What do you think?"

Cici narrowed her eyes. "Ted?" she demanded. "Are you serious? Is that really you?"

The laughter faded to a gentle smile. "It's Valerie now," she said. "People call me Val. And yes, it's really me. For the first time in my life."

To which Cici replied, "Oh. My. God."

A silence of about five seconds passed. Paul and Derrick looked stunned. Bridget looked incredulous.

Cici looked amazed. Everyone looked at Val. And Val merely looked expectant.

It was Harmony who finally spoke. "Pluto square Venus," she murmured. "Sex, secrets and deception." Then she smiled, making an obvious attempt not to look smug as she moved past them. "Well, then. I'd better get Purline out here with a broom and dustpan to clean up the mess."

She gave Val one last look, accompanied by an approving nod, and swept off toward the back of the house, caftan fluttering.

Paul said under his breath, "There'll be no living with her from now on."

Derrick ignored him, hurrying over to Val, his hands outstretched warmly. "Well!" he exclaimed. "This is wonderful! I mean, we just couldn't be happier, or prouder, or, well, happier!" He grasped both of Val's hands warmly even as he cast a rather desperate look over his shoulder to Paul. "I mean, this is just so… wonderful for you! Really!" He dropped his gaze to her beautifully manicured hands and added, apropos of nothing, "Love the nails."

He dropped her hands and backed away awkwardly.

Paul came quickly to his rescue. "Of course it is. Wonderful, that is. Well done, old man!—I mean of course, Te—Valerie, was it? Val! Good for you, really. Of course we're happy for you. It's just such a surprise. One hardly knows what to say, how to react. We're just all so…"

"Shocked," supplied Cici flatly.

Derrick nodded his consent. "That would be the word. Shocked. Wouldn't you say, Paul?"

"Shocked," agreed Paul.

"Oh, for heaven's sake, Ted!" Bridget burst out impatiently. "Why in the world didn't you tell us?"

"Val," corrected all four of them at once, just as Lindsay came out from the parlor.

"Tell us what?" she demanded. "Is Ted here?" She gave the stranger a polite smile and glanced around the foyer. "Where is he?" She noticed the broken glasses and spilled wine on the floor and added, "Oops. I told you not to try to carry all those glasses by yourself."

Cici gave her a resigned look, gestured wanly to Val, and said, "Lindsay, meet Val. You may once have known her as Ted."

Lindsay stared at Val for a beat. Val smiled broadly and assured Lindsay, "It's me."

Lindsay turned quickly back to Cici and Bridget. "Kiki is right behind me."

Val's face lit up. "Kiki's here already? I can't wait to see her! We've been texting, you know," she confided, laying a hand lightly on Lindsay's arm, "but this is the first time we've seen each other since... well, in years! This is going to be fabulous!"

She took an eager step forward, but Cici held out a staying hand. "Maybe not," she said.

Bridget looked at Val urgently. "Does Kiki know? Did you tell her?"

Val looked mildly flustered. "Well, of course she does! That is..." Color crept up her artfully made up cheeks. "Maybe not in so many words. I mean, not entirely. I wanted to surprise her..."

Alarm flashed around the group. "Oh, my God," groaned Derrick. "Kiki does *not* do well with surprises."

"This is not a surprise, this is a disaster," Lindsay said.

Derrick put it more succinctly. "She's going to implode."

"No one makes a scene like Kiki," agreed Paul. "Remember the Johnsons' party?"

A repressed shudder went around the group, and even Val looked concerned. "She does have a tendency to over react," she admitted.

"Over-react?" Cici stared at her. "She had Marianne Johnson arrested!"

Val looked less and less certain. "She's not going to like being the last to know."

Lindsay said, "Um, as much as I'd like to be here for this, I think I just remembered I left my flat iron on. Maybe I'll just read about it in the paper..."

Derrick groaned once more, pressing his hand to his heart, and Paul implored, mostly to himself, "Couldn't we have *one* nice event without the drama? Just one?"

"It's not just Kiki," Derrick agreed in dismay, "but the entire event! We promised our guests a weekend filled with romance and delight an instead we get..."

Words seemed to fail him, so Paul supplied glumly, "The eruption of Mount Kiki."

Derrick nodded, swallowing hard. "And we've got Miss Delaware already on her way and if that rack of lamb sits even one minute past seven o'clock it will be ruined and ...Oh dear, could the timing possibly be any worse?"

As though in answer to that question, Purline appeared with a broom and dustpan. "Hey ya'll," she said, snapping her gum. "That queen is here."

~6~

The next few moments were controlled chaos. Paul rushed to the window and peered out, half-hiding himself behind the frame. "Back limousine," he reported grimly, "liveried driver, enough matched luggage to see Eva Gabor through a world cruise... it's her, all right."

Kiki came out of the parlor and exclaimed, "There you are! I thought you'd gotten lost!"

Panic flashed around the group as Val drew a breath to speak. Paul whirled from the window. Derrick cast Val a desperate, pleading look and mouthed, *Not now.*

It looked for a moment as though Val might ignore him, but Cici grabbed her arm.

"Kiki," Cici exclaimed. "You won't believe it! This is an old friend from..." She looked at Val a little desperately, momentarily at a loss, but recovered smoothly. "From the old days! I haven't seen her in forever, couldn't believe my eyes! I was just going to show her to her room. You don't mind do you?"

She had barely finished speaking before Derrick pushed forward, declaring, "Kiki, just in time! She's here, Miss Delaware is here!" He grabbed the cheese tray from Bridget and thrust it into Kiki's hands. "Be a dear and tell the others, will you? I have simply got to go welcome our special guest!"

"But," sputtered Kiki, looking excitedly toward the window, "I want to say hello! I adore her books! I've been dying to tell her..."

"And you will, you will," Derrick assured her, trying to turn her back toward the parlor—and away from Val—with urgent little flapping motions of his hands. "But first—"

"Champagne!" cried Paul, clapping his hands together. "Purline, darling, chop-chop! Didn't I say champagne at 5:00?"

Purline, bent over the dustpan as she swept up shards of glass and spilled liquid, gave him a deadly look. Lindsay said quickly, "I'll get it." She hurried down the hall.

Kiki looked in confusion from the window to the tray in her hands. "But I really wanted to…"

Bridget gave her an affectionate pat on the shoulder and declared cheerfully, "Everyone helps out around here, Kiki, you don't mind, do you?" She noticed Val's suede overnight bag sitting on the floor by the reception desk and called, "Oh, Miss um, er, Val!" She grabbed the bag and rushed after Cici, who was ushering a somewhat reluctant looking Val down the corridor. "You forgot this!"

Derrick squeezed Kiki's arm. "Thank you for being such a dear! I'll bring Miss Delaware in for introductions just as soon as she's settled. Tell the others, won't you? Isn't this exciting?"

Kiki drew a breath for a reply but Derrick was already hurrying away, straightening his tie as he went. Kiki gave a small frown of irritation, then a shrug, and took the cheese tray into the parlor.

Paul swept open the door and the two men stepped out into the February dusk, broad smiles of welcome on their faces. Paul started down the steps but Derrick stopped him. "Wait," he said anxiously. "Is there a protocol? I mean, do we bow or curtsey or…"

Paul gave him an incredulous look. "To Miss Delaware? You do realize she's not a real queen, don't you?"

"The prince," returned Derrick impatiently. "I mean the prince! Prince… what was his name again? Oh dear, I can't believe I've forgotten the prince's name!"

"Prince Leon," supplied Paul.

"Do we call him by his first name?" Derrick pressed. "Prince Leon? How do we even address him? Sir? Your majesty? And come to think of it, if Miss Delaware is married to him, doesn't that make her a princess? So maybe we *do* bow to her! And do we call her 'ma'am' or 'your royal highness' or 'your majesty'? Because on *The Crown* sometimes the P.M. calls the queen 'ma'am' and sometimes 'your majesty' and I'm sure it's something similar for a princess. Oh, I should have asked her secretary when I had her on the phone! What was I thinking?"

Even Paul looked mildly perplexed over the dilemma, but only for a moment. The driver opened the back door of the limousine and a tall, lanky youth in a navy blue uniform and polished black boots got out.

"Good heavens," Derrick gasped involuntarily. "He's twelve years old!"

"Well," replied Paul, "that solves the problem of how to address him." And to Derrick's dismayed, questioning look he replied, "'Son' seems appropriate."

The young man was, in all likelihood, not twelve years old, but he certainly couldn't have been a day over twenty five. His wavy dark hair dipped enchantingly over one eyebrow, and his military uniform—complete with red sash and gold braid epaulets—looked like something out of a fairy tale. As the two men on the porch watched, somewhat transfixed, he turned to extend his hand to the woman in the car.

A gloved hand gripped his, and one foot, sensibly clad in a high-top sneaker, planted itself on the ground. Above that foot was a pink chiffon skirt accompanied by the hem of a fur coat. For a moment nothing happened. The prince tugged on her hand, then reached inside the car to grasp her other hand. The driver came forward to help. Both men tugged, shoulders straining. Paul and Derrick, scarcely able to contain their alarm, hurried down the steps to lend their assistance.

But by the time they reached the car the package had been delivered, like a calf from a cow, and Esmerelda Delaware tottered unsteadily to her sneaker-clad feet. Her face was a map of time coated in faintly rouged face powder and accented by ruby-painted lips, her pink feathered hat perched precariously atop a wreath of thin silver curls, and her earlobes dragged down by the weight of diamond pendant earrings. She smoothed the ruffled fur of her champagne colored mink coat, straightened the bodice of her beaded pink chiffon gown, and looked around imperiously. "This," she observed with a sniff, "doesn't look at all like Florida."

Derrick rushed forward, his hand extended. "Miss Delaware, welcome to the Hummingbird House! We're so honored to have you." He turned to her companion and added, "Your royal highness." He executed a sweeping bow from the waist. "Welcome."

"This is an incomparable thrill," Paul hastened to add, right behind him. "Our guests have talked of nothing else. They can't wait to meet you. But first, let's get you settled. How was your trip? Pleasant, I trust. We've been so fortunate with the weather. A bit nippy of course, but nothing like it can be this time of year."

She looked the two of them over without expression, and made no move to accept either of their offered hands. "Who the devil are you?" she demanded. She turned to the prince and insisted, "Who are these impudent young people?"

The prince looked down his long nose at them and drawled in reply, "I'm sure I have no idea." He had the faintest hint of an exotic, completely unidentifiable accent.

Derrick, still in a half-bow, said quickly, "A thousand pardons, ma'am, I mean Miss, er, that is, what I mean to say..."

Paul gave him a single disbelieving look before rushing to his rescue. "Miss Delaware, I'm Paul Slater and this is my partner, Derrick Anderson. We're your hosts for the weekend. If you need anything at all, just ask."

She considered this for a brief moment and then gave a sharp nod. "I'll have a Scotch and soda and be quick about it." She glared at Derrick. "Where's the bloody swimming pool?" She turned again to the prince, her voice turning querulous. "Weren't we promised a swimming pool?"

To which the prince replied once again, in a bored tone, "I'm sure I have no idea."

Paul lifted his arm and crooked a finger to the driver. "If you'll just follow me, my good man, I'll show you where to take the luggage. Derrick, would you like to show the, um, royal couple to their accommodations?"

Derrick managed, "Yes, of course. We've put you in the Magnolia Suite, adjoining rooms as you requested, our very finest accommodations, naturally."

"Naturally," murmured the prince, disinterested. "We will also require three orange slices and a glass of warm milk, 96 degrees Fahrenheit, and one ounce of dark chocolate, 72 percent cacao, to be brought to our rooms at precisely 10:45 this evening. And do be quick with the Scotch and soda, won't you? My lady does not like to be kept waiting." He offered his arm to the lady in question with a small incline of his head, and, when she took it he looked pointedly at Derrick. "Neither," he said, "do I."

Derrick trotted up the stairs and swung the door open with another theatrical sweep of his arm. "Your royal highnesses," he said, "after you."

The prince returned a disdainful look. "But of course." He started up the stairs, holding his elderly companion's elbow solicitously.

Esmerelda Delaware gave a disgruntled *harrumph* and tugged sharply at the collar of her fur coat. "This is really quite unacceptable, you know. I distinctly recall being told there were no stairs in Florida. Check my contract, won't you my dear? No stairs. It's a law."

It was at that moment that both men noticed Harmony standing in the shadow of the open door, wrapped in a colorful fringed shawl and wearing an expression of angelic innocence on her face. It almost would have been kinder if she'd said "I told you so" out loud, but of course there was no need. It was clear by now she had been right.

This was definitely shaping up to be a disaster.

~7~

Lindsay came into the room that had been assigned to Ted Butler—aka Val Butler—and closed the door firmly, leaning against it. All three women inside the room had been talking at once, but they broke off abruptly when she came in. Lindsay fixed Val with a stern stare and demanded, "First of all, what in the world is going on?"

"That's exactly what…" Bridget began.

"You took the words right out of…" said Cici at the same time.

Val said, "If you'd just give me a minute…"

"Secondly," Lindsay said, ignoring all of them, "I love your hair!" She pushed away from the door and came over to Val, examining her lustrous mane with admiration. "What is that color, Autumn Sunset? And how do you get it so glossy? You're prettier than I am. I think I hate you."

Val laughed and threw her arms around Lindsay. The two women hugged for a moment and then Val stepped away, her eyes misting a little as she looked around the group. "Oh, girls, I've missed you all! You always made me laugh. I've missed everyone, really. That's why I wanted this weekend to be so, well… special." Her smile began to fade, to be replaced by regret and apology. "I guess I blew that."

Cici looked at her with a mixture of helplessness and exasperation. "Look, I don't mean to be unsympathetic. I know this whole thing must have been hard for you. But how could you possibly have thought it would be a good idea to *surprise* everyone?"

She sighed and unbelted her coat, tossing it across the bench at the foot of the bed. She was wearing an emerald green Dolce Gabanna sheath that fit her in a way that caused the other three women to share a look of undisguised jealousy, to which Val was oblivious.

"I didn't," she admitted unhappily. "I didn't think it was a good idea. I just didn't know how else to handle this." She sank down into the floral wing chair by the fireplace and twisted her hands in her lap, looking up at them with a helpless shrug. "I've never told anyone before. You all are the first."

"Oh," said Cici, taken aback. "Well... we're flattered. I guess."

Bridget's face softened with compassion and she sat down on the edge of the bench, leaning forward. "No one? Not even your family?"

She shook her head slowly. "My parents are dead, and I don't have any siblings. I guess there are a few cousins scattered around, but we're not close. Living abroad for all those years, I kind of lost touch with friends, including you. Now when I meet people I'm just me, Val. No one knows who I used to be, and so far I haven't felt close enough to anyone to bring it up."

"Wow," said Lindsay softly. "You really did start a whole new life."

She nodded. "In a way it's been exciting. I mean, who gets a chance to do that? I feel so lucky. But in another way... it's lonely. Kiki was my anchor through everything, my only real friend, just like she's been my whole life. And now you're telling me she thinks I've been—I've been *deceiving* her the whole time?" She gave a fierce shake of her head and started to rise. "I've got to talk to her."

Cici waved her back down into her chair. "She doesn't think anything," she explained impatiently. "She doesn't even know you're here."

"Or," added Bridget, using both hands to indicate Val's transformed appearance, "who you are."

Cici pulled up a chair from the tole-painted escritoire in the corner and sat down in front of Val, effectively blocking her in. "I just don't understand," she said, "how the subject never came up in all of your correspondence back and forth. How could you *not* mention the most important decision of your life?"

"But I did!" Val insisted. "I mean I told her about my identity crisis…"

"Oh for heaven's sake." Lindsay rolled her eyes. "You said *identity* crisis, not *gender* crisis?"

Val blinked her impossibly long lashes a couple of times, beginning to understand. "Well, maybe I did. It's not as though you can write a thesis when you're texting, you know. But I told her about my therapy— you have to have counseling for a year before they'll approve you for surgery, you know-- and I sent her pictures. Look."

She dug into her purse and took out her phone, scrolling until she found the right text, then held out the phone triumphantly to Lindsay. On the screen was a picture of Val looking not quite as put-together as she did now: She was wearing a blond wig styled in a bob with dangling earrings and a black sequined evening gown. Her skin was a little coarser and her makeup not quite as subtly applied as it was now. But the precursor of the woman she was about to become was definitely there.

"That was right after I'd started hormone treatment," she explained. "I was trying to decide on a look."

Beneath the photo was the text: *What do you think?* And the reply from Kiki: *It's so you!*

Lindsay silently passed the phone to Cici who passed it to Bridget, who returned it to Val.

Cici said, "Look at the date."

Looking a little puzzled, Val glanced at the phone. "October 31."

"Kiki thought it was a Halloween costume," Bridget explained.

An immediate objection formed on Val's lips, then faded. She looked at the phone again, and sank back in her chair. "Oh," she said.

Lindsay gave a small shake of her head. "Just because you identify as a woman doesn't mean you stop thinking like a man, I guess. More's the pity."

Val looked both miffed and uncomfortable. "I don't know what you mean by that."

"I mean," retorted Lindsay, "that you were so busy worrying about yourself that it never even occurred to you to put yourself in Kiki's place. You just assumed she understood what was going on with you. You never actually bothered to tell her."

"Is it possible," Bridget put in gently, "that you were deliberately vague in your texts because you were, well, a little nervous about telling the truth?"

"All you had to do was dial her number and have an actual conversation, instead of typing out letters on a screen," added Cici.

"And," Lindsay said, "you went to an awful lot of trouble—even moving out of the country—to make sure you didn't have to explain yourself to anyone."

"It's not that we're judging," Cici said quickly. "It's just that, all things considered, maybe you shouldn't expect too much of Kiki when she, uh, learns about your decision."

"Which she never will unless I talk to her." Val set her shoulders in resolution and started once again to rise. "She might be a little upset with me at first, but it's really just a simple matter of miscommunication, anyone can see that. I know she'll understand."

"It's a little more than a 'simple' miscommunication," Lindsay said. "She's planning to propose to you."

Val stared at Lindsay, dumbfounded. "Propose what?"

"Marriage, you idiot," said Cici. "All those things you said about how much you loved her and that there'd never be another woman like her—what did you expect her to think?"

"But I do love her!" Val insisted. A slight haze of panic came into her eyes. "She's my best friend, I adore her, that's the way we talk to each other! And – wait a minute, she read you my texts?"

Cici waved a dismissive hand. "That's hardly the point. The point is—"

"The point is," put in Bridget mildly, "text messaging might not be the best way to discuss matters of the heart."

"Oh my goodness," Val said softly. "It never occurred to me. I guess she was so vulnerable after the divorce, and, Lindsay, you're right. I was completely wrapped up in my own troubles…"

"Not that there's anything wrong with that," Bridget hastened to assure her.

"I never even guessed she might have those kinds of feelings for me," Val admitted. She looked at the other women helplessly. "I don't know what to do. We're here now, and I thought she'd be happy for me. But instead this is going to destroy her. I just don't know what to do."

None of them had an immediate answer, and before anyone could even make an attempt to come up with one, there was a peremptory knock on the door. "Are you decent?" called Derrick.

Without waiting for a response, Paul pushed open the door and strode inside, declaring, "Who the devil cares? It's not as though we could be shocked by anything we see."

"Not after the day we've had," Derrick agreed, following. "Oh my dears, you just will not believe it!"

"Everything all settled here?" Paul demanded. Cici drew a breath to reply but he went on, "Good, because we've got bigger problems." He went over to the decanter of sherry that was displayed on the bedside table and poured two glasses, handing one to Derrick. "My God, do you think she was drunk?"

"Who?" Cici managed to put in.

"Esmerelda Delaware, that's who," replied Derrick, and downed his sherry in one gulp. Paul refilled his glass. "Oh my God, I think that was a mink she was wearing. A *real* one. We have animal lovers here!"

"I'm an animal lover," Bridget volunteered.

"And that *hat*," Paul said, suppressing a shudder. "The feathers were dusty! Can we even talk about her sneakers?"

"No," Derrick replied firmly. "We cannot."

"I love Esmerelda Delaware's novels," Val said, a little wistfully. "Remember *Love Long Lost*, girls?"

"Oh," Lindsay said, pressing her hand to her heart, "that speech Eric DuFaustier gave just before he leapt overboard, promising to come back for her…"

"And then when he did, all those years later," Bridget added, her voice tightening with emotion, "he was in a wheelchair!"

The three women shared a tender smile. "Gosh, we had some good times at book club, didn't we?" said Lindsay.

"Ladies please," interrupted Paul, "you're straying from the point!"

"Which is?" inquired Cici.

Derrick looked at her in exasperation. "The point is that in less than twenty four hours the heavily advertised and widely acclaimed Esmerelda Delaware, perhaps *the* most celebrated romance novelist of our time, is scheduled to give a speech to our guests and I'm not entirely sure she can remember her own name!"

"And we haven't even told them about the prince," Derrick said morosely. "I'm not even sure he's of legal drinking age, and we just got our liquor license back, you know." He looked anxious. "Should we cancel the wine with dinner?"

"Don't be ridiculous," replied Paul impatiently. "It's a food and wine *pairing*. What do you suggest we serve? Lemonade?"

Val said, "Guys, it looks as though you've got your hands full and I don't want to cause you any more problems. I think the best thing for me to do is just leave."

There was a wave of protest, but Val raised a staying hand as she stood. "No, seriously, this was a bad idea. I should have thought it through. It's not fair to do this to you, and it's definitely not fair to do this to

Kiki. So I think the best thing for me to do is to head home. I'll text Kiki on the way."

"You'll do no such thing!" cried Cici.

"She came all the way from Colorado!" Lindsay objected.

And Bridget added, "Haven't we agreed that text messaging is definitely not the way to handle this?"

"Oh, my dear." Derrick look pained as he placed a reassuring hand on her arm. "This was supposed to be your big moment and we've ruined it. Don't listen to us. We're selfish brutes, both of us."

"This isn't like us, really," Paul insisted sincerely. "We think your news is thrilling and we want to support you in every possible way. Clearly there are far more significant issues here than whether or not our celebrity guest speaker is a drunken cradle-robber."

"I don't know," Val said uneasily. "That sounds fairly significant to me."

"You need to talk to Kiki in person," Bridget insisted gently.

"You've been putting it off for five years," Lindsay pointed out.

"And you don't know when you'll get another chance," Cici agreed.

"The ladies are absolutely right, of course," Paul said with authority. "And we're honored that you chose the Hummingbird House for your big reveal, as it were. Only we were wondering if, given Kiki's volatility…"

"Which has always been one of the things we love about her," Derrick put in quickly.

"And the delicate nature of the subject," Paul went on, "we were wondering if it would be too much to ask…" He looked at Derrick for guidance.

"If you could postpone the conversation until after dinner," Derrick provided. "After all, we do have other guests…"

"That sweet couple from Montreal," Paul supplied. "And the Browns, celebrating their anniversary…"

"And the rack of lamb cost a fortune," Derrick confided.

"Not to mention the Montrachet we planned to serve with it," Paul said. "We just want everyone to have a nice evening. Maybe…" He glanced again at Derrick. "Morning would be soon enough?"

Val looked uncertain. "I don't know. She's expecting me to be here tonight."

"You could text her that you're running late," Paul said. "That way she won't worry."

"And for tonight you could go on pretending to be Cici's friend from the old days," Derrick supplied hopefully.

Val said, "I don't like to lie."

"Oh my darling," said Paul gently. "You've been living a lie for fifty years. What difference can one more night possibly make?"

Cici shot Paul a sharp look and Lindsay objected, "Oh, for heaven's sake! This is crazy."

Bridget agreed, "I don't know, boys. This doesn't sound like a very good idea to me."

"It sounds," Cici said flatly, "like a really *bad* idea. These things never work out, and it's not fair of you to ask a friend to tell a giant lie to someone she cares about just to save your rack of lamb."

Both Paul and Derrick looked properly chastised. Paul admitted unhappily, "You're right of course. I apologize, Val. It's just that…"

"No, wait," Val said. She gave a single decisive shake of her head. "This is my problem, and there's no reason to ruin everyone else's weekend. I won't lie to Kiki, but I won't tell her the truth tonight, either. I'll text her and tell her I'll see her in the morning. Just don't seat me next to her at dinner okay?"

"Absolutely not," Derrick assured her.

"No problem whatsoever," added Paul.

"I don't like this," Lindsay said.

"Me either." Bridget looked at Val meaningfully. "No good ever comes from hiding from the truth."

Val tried to hide her discomfort. "I'm not hiding from the truth," she said, "just postponing it a little."

"It's a disaster," pronounced Cici, "waiting to happen."

Paul and Derrick looked at each other, and then at the ladies. "Disasters we can handle," Derrick assured them.

Paul finished off his sherry and added grimly, "It's the outright catastrophes we're trying to avoid."

~*~

The Hummingbird House
Book Lovers Valentine's Eve Dinner Menu

Miniature Maryland crab cakes with red pepper
pesto

~

Asparagus soup served with parmesan crisps

~

Goat-cheese biscuits served with honey butter

~

Grilled hearts of palm and cherry tomato salad with
bleu cheese and raspberry vinaigrette

~

Roast garlic and herb-crusted rack of lamb served
on a bed of root vegetables
with minted au jus sauce

~

Sweetheart strawberry tartlets served in a dark
chocolate shell and topped with crème fraiche

~*~

~8~

The dining room of the Hummingbird House was actually a glassed-in porch that overlooked the gardens and, in daylight hours, offered an inspirational view of the mountains in the distance. Even in the dark, the view was enchanting: the garden paths were softly up lit, branches of Japanese cherry and kumquat trees artfully wrapped in fairy lights, and the dancing waters of the central fountain were cleverly enhanced by mood lighting that, in honor of the occasion, faded from pink to rose to sparkling red wine.

For large parties, breakfasts, and the Hummingbird House's famous Sunday brunch, the porch was furnished with round tables seating four to six, each draped in floor-length tablecloths and boasting individual floral centerpieces. Tonight, in order to give everyone equal access to their celebrity guest, the seating was family style. One large oval table was placed in the center of the room, covered in an ivory cloth and dressed with nosegays of red roses and white candles in cut-glass globes running down the center of the table. There were "oooh"s and "ahh"s from appreciative guests as they entered the room.

Paul stationed himself at the entrance to greet the diners while Derrick paced anxiously outside the Magnolia room, ready to escort their royal highnesses to dinner and muttering prayers under his breath to St. Valentine that their celebrity guest would actually be sober enough to make it out of her room. Cici, Bridget and Lindsay, who had not had to change for dinner, were on time and remarkably relaxed, given the circumstances. They brought their champagne glasses and took their places at the table behind their name cards, but they had barely had time to take a single sip before Paul called first Bridget, and then Lindsay away. "So sorry," he said to Cici, leaning over the back of her chair. "Harmony's off on another one of her wild hare chases, Skyping with someone in Japan about the conjunction of the moon and Mars, and I just need to borrow the girls for a minute. You will be a dear and keep an eye on the Kiki situation won't you? I rely on you!"

"Why me?" Cici protested. "I told you, I'm totally against the whole thing."

But Kiki had already arrived at the entrance to the dining room, holding her phone and looking anxious and unhappy. Paul told Cici, "Darling, I don't know how I'd manage without you!" And he hurried off to greet Kiki.

"I just got a message from Ted," she told Paul, frowning. "He says he'll see me at breakfast. What do you think that means? So I texted him back and asked if everything is okay, and he just said 'Don't worry, everything is fine.' What do you think that means?"

"I think that means don't worry, everything is fine," Paul replied in a soothing tone. He touched her shoulder lightly as he gestured to the table. "Honestly, I'll never grasp the appeal of all this texting back and forth. So much is lost in translation, don't you think? Here you go, my dear, I've seated you next to Cici and across from our guest of honor who..." he cast an anxious glance over his shoulder, wringing his hands once, "will be here momentarily, I'm sure. Let me get you a glass of wine."

Purline, who was being paid double overtime to wear a black skirt and white blouse while she served, came from the kitchen in scuffed white sneakers and announced, "I put the crab cakes in the warming oven, but they won't hold more than another ten minutes."

Paul waved her away distractedly. "Very well, my dear, you can serve as soon as our guests of honor get here." He took a wine glass down from the rack over the antique marble-topped buffet and poured from one of the bottles that was uncorked and waiting there.

She looked at him curiously. "So let me ask you something. That queen, she's married to a prince, right? So what's he the prince *of*? And is she a queen or a princess?"

Paul looked at her blankly for a moment, then recovered himself with a blink. "Purline, my darling, I simply do not have time to explain to you the intricacies of a foreign peerage right now. So be a dear and scurry back to the kitchen, will you? Whatever you do, do not let the crab cakes die!" He hurried off to serve Kiki's wine.

Purline rolled her eyes at his retreating back and turned to saunter back to the kitchen, muttering, "They was alive and kicking when I left them."

The room began to fill with soft laughter and murmurs of excited anticipation as the guests arrived, singly and in couples, and found their seats. The chatter was mostly about their guest of honor: "I saw pictures of her castle in Scotland," said one. "Unbelievable!" Another added, "I thought this latest book was her best yet, didn't you?" And another, in a more hushed tone, said, "I had no idea she was so old. I guess we're lucky to get to meet her now, before she, well, you know."

When Kiki slid into her chair beside Cici, Cici asked cheerfully, "Did you get to meet her yet? Miss Delaware, I mean. What did you think?"

Kiki shrugged and sipped her wine. "She went to her room to rest before dinner. I don't think anyone got to talk to her. I got a look at the prince, though. He looked like he just climbed out of Cinderella's carriage. Did you hear Ted isn't coming? Not to dinner anyway. He'll be here by morning."

Cici managed to keep a straight face. "Oh. That's a shame." She picked up her wine glass.

Kiki sighed. "I'm so disappointed. I know we still have most of the weekend, but still…Oh." She looked over Cici's shoulder. "There's your friend. Wow, she looks great. I wish I could wear things like that."

Val was wearing a form fitted red silk dress with a bold splash of pink cherry blossoms running diagonally from décolletage to hem. Her hair was pulled to the side with a pink enameled barrette and cascaded gracefully over the opposite shoulder. She wore gold hoop earrings and a delicate gold chain with a small diamond heart around her neck. She looked like someone who thoroughly enjoyed her womanhood, and, watching her, Cici had to smile.

"She does have a flair," Cici agreed, sipping her wine.

"Oh dear," Kiki said. "I don't think she can find her seat. Do you want her to sit here? Should I move down?"

Val was moving around the table, glancing at place cards, but everyone had been seated except the hosts and the guests of honor. Cici swallowed quickly. "It was a last-minute reservation," she said. "Paul and Derrick must have forgotten to make a card."

"That's odd," said Kiki. "They're usually so meticulous." She lifted her hand to Val. "Come sit here," she said, beckoning to the empty place beside her.

Val glanced uncertainly at Cici, but there really was no choice. All the other places were taken. Cici reached across Kiki and turned the place card with Ted's name on it face-down as Val came around the table.

"My date bailed on me," Kiki explained when Val reached them. "There's an extra place." She extended her hand. "I'm Kiki."

Val looked at Cici, who returned a small, helpless shrug and took a quick sip of her wine. "I'm Valerie," she said, and shook Kiki's hand. "People call me Val."

Kiki tilted her head as she looked at her, her smile now mitigated by curiosity. "Where have I met you before? I swear I know you."

Cici choked a little on her wine and Val withdrew her hand from Kiki's grasp, tugging her hair a little more over the side of her face as she sat down. "Do you spend much time in California?"

"Gracious, no. Is that where you're from? I just can't get over how familiar you look."

Val turned the place card face-up again in a clumsy attempt to change the subject. "Your date?" she inquired, indicating the card.

Kiki nodded. "Ted. We haven't seen each other in awhile, but this was going to be a special night for us. You see…"

Cici said quickly, and rather loudly, "Oh, look! I think Miss Delaware is here!"

Everyone turned in their seats to watch as Paul and Derrick, looking as nervous as they were pleased, escorted the elegantly clad prince—black boots polished, sash pressed, and wearing a few more shiny medals than he had been upon arrival—and the equally well-attired Miss Delaware into the room. She wore a floor length white lace gown with ballet flats and evening gloves, and she held herself with the stiff-necked determination of someone who has grave doubts about her ability to take another unassisted step. Her gaze was regal, if somewhat glazed, and she smiled over the crowd in a faintly superior, carefully controlled fashion, as though she was afraid of smudging her lipstick, which already had begun to bleed into the crevices around her mouth.

Paul tapped a spoon against a crystal wine glass for attention. "Ladies and gentlemen, we are so privileged to have as our special guests this evening Prince Leon of... of..." Confused, he turned to the prince. "I'm terribly sorry," he murmured. "But I don't believe I ever heard anyone mention the name of your principality."

The prince stepped forward, his chin in the air. "I regret to say," he announced, "that my small but great nation is no more. Nonetheless, its royal family endures."

"Oh," said Paul, blinking. "Well, that's splendid."

"Good lord," murmured Val, lifting her glass to hide her words. "The prince looks as though he should be standing beside a pumpkin drawn by six white horses."

Kiki smothered a giggle behind her fingers. "I said the same thing!" she whispered back.

The two women shared a smile as Paul went on, "And of course the woman of the hour, author of over twenty-two of our very favorite books, winner of far too many awards to name, the reigning Queen of Romance, Miss Esmerelda Delaware!"

He stepped back to lead the room in a round of applause, and everyone got to their feet. The royal couple accepted the adulation that was their due with gracious nods of their heads. Kiki leaned into Val and murmured, "How in the world do you suppose she ever got that child to marry her?"

"She's got to be richer than God," Val replied. "Every prince has his price."

Kiki burst into giggles again.

"Did you read her latest?" Kiki asked as they resumed their seats.

"*Love Lay Dying?*" Val clasped a hand over her heart. "I think it's my favorite of them all! When Arabella gets the note stamped with the symbol of the black thorn..."

"And she doesn't even know the Black Thorn Raider is her own lover!" exclaimed Kiki.

"I can't believe I left my copy at home," said Val. "I was so looking forward to getting it autographed. Say what you will about the author," she added with a sigh, "but her books are phenomenal. They just seem to get better and better."

Kiki smiled at her. "So how did you end up alone on Valentine's Day, Val? It's just the pits, isn't it? Did your guy stand you up too?"

"Oh, I don't know about that," Val responded smoothly, ignoring her last question for the first. "I rather like traveling alone. You get to keep your own schedule, go where you want to, dine when you want to, do what you want to, and..." She lifted her wine glass to Kiki. "You meet the most interesting people."

Kiki replied a little wistfully, "I don't think I'm very good at being alone."

"Maybe you haven't given it a proper chance."

Kiki smiled a little and admitted, "Maybe. I was married for a long time."

"The first step," advised Val, "is learning to appreciate your own company. I spent most of my life going from one relationship to another, but it wasn't until I learned to love and value myself for who I was that I was really happy."

Cici leaned forward and said, a little too enthusiastically, "So! What's everyone reading?"

"I've been going back over Esmerelda Delaware's earlier books," Kiki said, "so I wouldn't sound too dumb at the lecture tomorrow. Do you remember *Love's Last Chance*? The one where the baby is found on the chapel steps and he turns out to be..."

"The duke's half brother and the king's heir!" replied Val before Cici could. "Oh, I loved that one. It was one of the first books we read in..." She caught the flash of warning in Cici's eyes and finished smoothly, "My old reading group."

"Ours too!" exclaimed Kiki. "Afterwards we talked about taking a group trip to Cornwall but we never did."

"Oh, I adore Cornwall," Val said warmly. "You must go, you really must. But be sure to make the trip in the summer. The winters are beyond miserable."

Kiki laughed. "That's funny, my friend Ted said the same thing. He was there a couple of summers ago and sent me the most gorgeous photos. When were you there?"

Val lifted her glass and replied carefully, "Oh, quite some time ago. I'm sure it's changed since then. Do you get much chance to travel, Kiki?"

Cici tried to relax as Lindsay slid into the chair next to her and whispered, "How's it going?"

Cici slid a sideways glance at Kiki and Val, who were deep in conversation about something Cici couldn't quite make out. There was a lot of laughter involved, though, so she tried not to worry. "So far so good, I guess," she said. "Where have you been?"

"Bridget volunteered to make the sauce for the lamb, which meant I was on duty outside Miss Delaware's door in case she popped a button or something." Lindsay snapped open her napkin and spread it in her lap. "You realize we're only invited to these things for the free labor, don't you?"

"That's not nice." Cici wrestled back a smile as she sipped her wine. "It's true, but not nice."

Paul and Derrick went around the table pouring wine while Purline served the first course, and when Derrick reached Cici he whispered, "What *happened?*" He made big eyes toward the couple sitting on Cici's left. "I thought the plan was to keep them apart!"

"I think it's okay," Cici replied. "Anyway, you're the ones who forgot to make a new place card. How's the guest of honor?"

He smothered a groan as he poured her wine. "I think she's hammered. She hasn't said a word." He moved to Kiki's glass, returning his voice to its normal tone. "Here's a playful little Calvet Alsace pinot blanc. It pairs beautifully with the crispy crab cakes and the sweetness of the pesto. Notice the hint of apples in the bouquet." He pushed his luck by adding, "Are you having a good time, Kiki? I was so sorry to hear Ted couldn't join us tonight."

Kiki smiled and lifted her glass to Val in a salute. "I'm having a wonderful time, Derrick. Thanks for asking. It's always nice to meet new friends."

Derrick murmured, "Yes, isn't it?" And he hurried off as the two women clinked glasses.

The crab cakes were delicious, the pinot blanc was as playful as promised, and if the appetizer course was any indication the evening was off to an excellent start.

By the time the soup bowls were removed, Kiki and Val were chatting like the closest of confidants. Bridget had taken her place at the table with the rest of the guests, and after sampling two wine pairings, the conversation around the table was relaxed, the laughter easy. The prince, at the opposite end of the table from Cici, met Paul's and Bridget's attempt at conversation with monosyllabic replies. Esmerelda Delaware, who was only a few seats away at Derrick's right, concentrated studiously on her meal and, as far as Cici could tell, had yet to say anything to anyone.

Cici nudged Lindsay with her elbow, then nodded toward the guest of honor. "Do you think we're allowed to talk to her?"

"A few people have tried," Lindsay whispered back, "but she doesn't answer. Maybe she forgot to put in her hearing aids?"

Cici was about to reply when there was a burst of laughter from the couple to her left. Val declared, dropping an affectionate hand atop Kiki's arm, "You are a kick, Kiki! I can't remember when I've laughed so much!" She lifted her glass to Kiki in a salute, eyes twinkling. "Kicky Kiki."

The amusement in Kiki's face faded into a kind of curious intensity as she examined Val's face. "That's so strange. The only other person who's ever called me that was ..." And she looked down at the place card in front of Val's plate, her puzzlement turning into a frown.

Lindsay gripped Cici's arm in a panic, her wide eyes telegraphing, *Do something!*

"Miss Delaware!" Cici practically shouted the words, leaning across the table to get the older woman's attention.

She got everyone's attention except the woman she was addressing. People interrupted their own conversations and turned their heads toward Cici politely. Derrick looked frozen with trepidation. Paul stopped pouring wine. Even Purline stopped delivering salad plates. Everyone waited.

A little desperately, Cici repeated, "Miss Delaware I was wondering…"

Esmerelda Delaware looked at Cici curiously, and for a moment Cici couldn't think of a single thing to say.

"Lord Whitleton," she blurted. "Yes, that's it. I was wondering where you got the inspiration for Lord Whitleton in *Love's Last Chance.*"

Miss Delaware smiled politely. "Who, dear?"

"The hero of your fourth book," Cici explained. "Lord Whitleton."

"I'm afraid I don't know the chap," replied the other woman. She picked up her empty glass, glancing around. "Is there more wine?"

Paul hurried to refill her glass and Lindsay volunteered, "He's the one who stole the heart of Lady Carolina when she was only thirteen. Lord Whitleton."

Esmerelda Delaware gave a delicate sniff in response. "Sounds like a bloody pedophile to me."

There was a shocked silence, and then the kind of uneasy laughter that often follows when listeners are uncertain whether a joke was, in fact, a joke.

From the other end of the table the prince remarked, "I think it is important to recall that those were very different times we speak of. Perhaps tomorrow we will discuss all these matters."

Cici sat back in her chair and picked up her wine glass, forcing a smile. "Sounds good to me."

"I know who you are!" Kiki exclaimed suddenly, staring at Val.

Cici froze with her glass halfway to her lips. Lindsay held her breath. Even Derrick, overhearing, didn't move.

"That woman in the beauty bar commercial!" Kiki declared, and turned to Cici. "You know who I mean!" She twisted back to Val excitedly. "That's it, isn't it? That's why you look so familiar!"

Val demurred, "That's kind of you to say, but…"

"She gets that a lot," Cici put in quickly. "The resemblance really is remarkable."

Derrick cast her a grateful look and turned to the guest of honor. "How did you meet the prince, Miss Delaware?"

"Who, dear?"

"Prince Leon," repeated Derrick, speaking loudly enough so that the whole table could hear. "Your husband."

Purline set the salad plate before her, and Esmerelda Delaware looked at it with satisfaction. "Toads," she declared. "My favorite." She stabbed at a cherry tomato with her salad fork. "The important thing, you know, is never to eat the heads."

No one seemed to know whether it was a joke this time, and this time no one laughed. Paul broke the tension with a stiff smile as the guest of honor shoved the tomato into her mouth. "Excellent advice, I'm sure we can all agree," he said. "Ladies and gentlemen, we have for you now a lovely hearts of palm salad with raspberry dressing and toasted pine nuts, accompanied by a Napa Valley rosé'..."

Lindsay whispered to Cici, "Do you think she's had a stroke?"

Cici replied unhappily, "At least one."

"Oh dear," murmured Kiki to Val. "I think Lindsay may be right. Our guest speaker may have problems that a good night's sleep won't be able to fix."

"I hope you're wrong," Val said. "I was looking forward to talking to her tomorrow. Her love stories have been such a big part of my life."

"I know. Mine too." Kiki smiled at her again. "I think it might be your eyes," she said suddenly. "There's just something so familiar about them. Honestly, I feel as though I've known you forever."

Val dropped her gaze. "Kiki," she said, "there's something I want to..."

"And so," declared Paul boisterously, dropping a firm hand on Val's shoulder, "what do you think of the rosé? It's a bit flowery for my taste, but it sets off the vinaigrette wonderfully, and there is a certain something to be said for a California wine, don't you agree?"

Val had no choice but to smile politely, sip the wine, and agree. She turned her attention to the guest of honor across the table. "Miss Delaware, I understand you have a castle in Scotland."

"Indeed I do." She gave a decisive nod of her head. "It has a dragon, you know."

Val lifted an eyebrow. "Does it?"

"Oh, yes. He's really quite fierce. Name's Igor." She stabbed another tomato.

Other diners glanced at Miss Delaware, glanced at each other, and finally decided the safest place for their attention was on their plates. But Val leaned forward with interest. "You don't see many dragons these days," she said. "How did the two of you become acquainted?"

For a moment Esmerelda just looked at Val, her rheumy blue eyes revealing nothing. And then she picked up her knife and fork, cut a precise section of artichoke heart, and said, "As a matter of fact, it is a rather amusing story…"

The one thing that could be said for the meal, everyone would later agree, was that the lamb was excellent. Throughout the main course, Val kept Esmerelda Delaware engaged in what were generally unintelligible conversations. Occasionally others would try to join in, only to flounder and retreat, but Val always rescued the moment. When Purline took away the entrée dishes and prepared to serve dessert, Kiki touched Val's hand and said softly, "This is so kind of you. I think the reason she hasn't said anything all evening is because no one knew how to talk to her. My Ted is like that. He knows just how to make people feel at ease."

Val smiled uncertainly and started to reply but Cici interrupted, keeping her voice low as well. "The prince looks worried, though. It must be difficult for him, especially out in public."

But even as she spoke, the prince stood and said something to Paul. Paul protested, "But we have a lovely dessert!"

The prince smiled regretfully, bowed and came to stand behind Esmerelda Delaware's chair. Derrick immediately got to his feet. The prince nodded his head at him. "I thank you for a most enjoyable evening. But now I regret to say it is time for us to retire. We have an important day ahead."

Derrick murmured a protest but there was no denying the relief on his face. The others at the table offered up regretful, sympathetic and somewhat embarrassed smiles, then turned studiously back to their drinks.

The prince placed his hands on the back of Miss Delaware's chair. "Come along, my lady. It's time to make our adieus."

She looked up at him querulously. "Where are we going? Oh, I do hope it's Florida."

She rose and took the prince's arm, nodded her head graciously to those she passed as he escorted her around the table toward the door. "It's been a lovely evening," she said, "and I so have enjoyed your companionship. Especially that of the gentleman in the red dress."

Everyone else gave indulgent little smiles as she stopped behind Val's chair, but Derrick, Cici and Lindsay froze. Val did not look up.

Esmerelda Delaware leaned across Val's shoulder and picked up the place card beside her glass, squinting as she read it. "Ted, is it? Well, Ted." She offered her hand. "I have thoroughly enjoyed our conversation."

The resignation—and the truth—in Val's eyes were clear for anyone to see as she stood. Kiki's smile faded. Her eyes grew still. Val took Esmerelda Delaware' fingers and bowed her head in a brief gesture of respect. "As did I, Miss Delaware."

Kiki did not take her eyes off Val as she resumed her seat. Around the table the murmur of conversation picked up again as the guests of honor departed and

Purline began to serve the dessert. At their little corner, no one moved, no one spoke.

Val said softly, "I'm sorry, Kiki. I wanted to tell you earlier. It's me. It's Ted."

Kiki did not react.

Cici said, "Kiki, I think the important thing to remember is that she's still the same person."

"And this kind of thing is much more common than you might imagine," Derrick rushed in. "Nothing to make a scene about at all. If you think about it, this is really a teaching moment. A wonderful opportunity to demonstrate our compassion, and tolerance, and…"

"And it wasn't his—her idea not to tell you," Lindsay put in urgently. "Honestly. We just wanted the evening to go smoothly, that's all."

"And," Val said sincerely, covering Kiki's hand with her own. "I didn't stand you up. I would never do that."

Kiki pulled her hand away and reached for her wine glass. "Good heavens, everyone!" She gave a light laugh that had only the faintest trace of wildness about it at the edge. "Are you kidding me? Did you think I didn't know? Of course I did. I was just playing along because I didn't think you wanted anyone else to know." She drained what was left in the glass and turned to Val, her voice bright. "You look fabulous, by the way. I can't wait to hear all about it." Again she laughed as Purline put the strawberry tart before her. "I can't believe you all thought I didn't know." She picked up her fork and added, "My goodness, doesn't this look amazing?"

But just as everyone was starting to breathe a sigh of relief—and share looks of cautious wonder at their good fortune—Kiki put her fork down with a clatter.

"I don't know what I'm thinking," she said. Her voice was beginning to sound brittle. "I can't possibly eat another bite. And I have to lose five pounds before the end of the month! So I believe I'd better call it a night. Will you all excuse me?"

Abruptly, she slid back her chair and strode out of the room.

Val said, "Kiki, wait!" She hurried after her, high heels clacking on the ancient oak floors.

Cici said flatly, "She didn't know."

Derrick sank down into his chair, letting his head fall back. "Jesus," he said, "take me now."

~*~

From The Happy Traveler *blog*
February 14

Nothing says Happy Valentine's Day like a charming country inn, a fire crackling in the fireplace, and a homemade scone. Early risers will find hot coffee, a pot of Earl Gray, and a basket of warm scones awaiting them in the reception parlor, along with one or more of our genial hosts, solicitous as always for our comfort. As the morning progresses the aromas from the kitchen become more and more enticing as the inimitable Purline—who will inform anyone who cares to listen that breakfast is her specialty—prepares for the buffet which is served from 8:00-10:00 AM. There is the usual fresh fruit, yogurt and toasted granola, along with a variety of breakfast breads(I highly recommend the orange cinnamon rolls!) for those who prefer a simple fare. Made to order are baked apples served with almond muesli, banana pancakes with warm maple syrup and toasted walnuts, and Belgian Waffles served with cherry compote (to die for!). There is also an amazing egg-and-mushroom frittata topped with sautéed asparagus and candied bacon that could be proudly served in any restaurant in New York. I confess my diet has hit a slight bump in the road this weekend, but that's what Valentine's Day is for, isn't it? Thank heavens lunch has been foregone in favor of an afternoon tea honoring our guest speaker.

One cautionary note, dear readers: Valentine's Day is not always the happiest of times for everyone. Someone you know may feel glum today, or all alone, or unloved. Maybe that someone is you. Do me a favor, will you my dears? Send yourself flowers. Eat a box of chocolates. Dance like no one is watching. Brighten everyone's day: show yourself some love.

~9~

"I waited outside her door until almost midnight," Val told Paul and Derrick unhappily the next morning. "She never answered my knock. I must have texted her a dozen times, but I guess she turned off her phone."

It was a little after 6:00 AM, and Paul, Derrick and Val were the only ones in the parlor. They stood before the fireplace, sipping coffee from sleek glass mugs that were etched with the inn's signature hummingbird. Derrick nibbled on a warm scone; Val had barely tasted hers.

"I feel responsible," Paul said.

"We do," Derrick corrected.

Paul nodded agreement. "We never should have asked you to keep your identity a secret. It was a plan doomed to failure."

"And," sighed Derrick, "Miss Delaware is our punishment."

Val shook her head sadly. "No, I brought this on myself. It was a stupid plan, coming here to surprise everyone. But the stupidest part was what I did to Kiki. I just wish she'd let me tell her how sorry I am."

"Maybe," Derrick suggested softly, lifting his coffee cup toward the window that overlooked the winter garden, "this is your chance."

Val turned to follow his gaze. Kiki was sitting on the edge of the stone fountain, wrapped in a puffer coat and wool scarf, absently tossing bits of gravel into the water. Val took a breath and squared her shoulders in resolution. "Wish me luck," she said.

She started toward the door, then turned back and poured another cup of coffee, adding sugar and a measure of cream. Carrying both cups, she made her way out to the garden.

Derrick sighed as he watched her go. "Well, this weekend couldn't have turned out worse, could it? Next time we'll listen to Harmony."

"Bite your tongue," Paul said, sipping his coffee. But he didn't look any happier than Derrick. In a moment he added, "What shall we do about the tea this afternoon? Specifically, our guest speaker."

"Maybe it's not as bad as we think," Derrick offered, though he didn't sound very hopeful. "Everyone knows artists are eccentric."

Paul gave Derrick a level look. "Esmerelda Delaware," he told him, "is more than eccentric."

"We could try talking to her," Derrick suggested. "Perhaps if we explained how much our guests have counted on being able to talk to her about her books, and how important it is that she try to answer their questions…"

"In words that actually go together in the same sentence," Paul specified. His tone was anything but optimistic.

Derrick sighed and lowered his gaze to his coffee cup. "Right."

"Well," said Paul after another moment's thoughtfulness, "I really don't see that we have a choice. We promised a weekend with Esmerelda Delaware and we must deliver—whether or not she's actually coherent."

"There were times last evening when she was quite entertaining," Derrick offered. "Perhaps it's the kind of thing that comes and goes."

"It's possible," admitted Paul. "If so, we can only hope it 'goes' by teatime this afternoon. Otherwise, we are definitely going to be in what one of Miss Delaware's characters would call a pickle."

"Gentlemen," said a voice from the doorway, "perhaps I can help."

Paul and Derrick turned as Prince Leon came into the room. He was dressed in jeans and a Harvard sweatshirt; his hair was tousled and his chin bore the faintest trace of stubble. He looked, if possible, even younger than he had yesterday.

"Prince Leon," said Paul said quickly, gesturing him in. "Good morning. Come in. We have coffee ready, or tea if you prefer."

And Derrick chimed in, "I hope you slept well, your highness. Do try one of the scones."

The young man's smile was tinged with weariness, suggesting that he had not, in fact, slept very well at all. He said, "First of all," he said, "I am not a prince. You may call me Leon. And secondly…" He looked from one to the other of them with an expression of rueful apology. "Esmerelda Delaware is not my wife. She's my grandmother."

~10~

Kiki did not look up as Val approached, and accepted the cup Val offered her without quite meeting her eyes. After a moment she took a sip and murmured, "Two sugars, a splash of cream. You remembered."

Val said, "I've been making your coffee almost since you were old enough to drink it."

"So you have."

Val sat beside her on the stone apron of the fountain, not too close. "It's cold," she remarked, for lack of anything better.

"Not so bad. The water makes it seem colder."

"I suppose."

"You should get a coat."

Val said quietly, "Kiki, I am so sorry. I know how this must make you feel, but I swear to you I'd never do anything to hurt you, or make you feel foolish, and I can't let you leave here thinking that's what was going on. The truth is…" She took a deep breath. "You are the most important person in my life. The person who's known me longest, the only one who matters. And telling you…I just didn't know how. I guess I was afraid."

Kiki stared at her, a touch of incredulity in her eyes. "Of what?"

"I'm not sure. Of things changing between us. Of losing you. Maybe of not losing you. You're the strongest connection I have to the person I used to be. It's easier to start over when you don't have to keep looking back. But mostly…" Another breath. "That you wouldn't approve. That you wouldn't like me now."

Kiki shook her head slowly. "Oh Ted," she said softly. "You should have known better than that."

"One of the things my therapist emphasized was how important it was to share my decision with the people closest to me," Valerie went on. "You're the only person I've ever been really close to. The only one I cared about. And the thing is, you're the one who actually gave me the courage to make the transition, back when I was in crisis and struggling with what I wanted the rest of my life to look like. I knew something had to change. You convinced me it was time to act."

Kiki made a small, mirthless sound that might have been an attempt at laughter. "I thought you were trying to decide whether or not to move to Europe." She lifted her coffee cup to her lips again.

Valerie said, "It doesn't matter. You knew I was trying to make a major life decision and you were there for me. You made me feel like someone was on my side. And I wanted to tell you. I *tried* to tell you, or pretended to tell you, with stupid little hints and euphemisms. And after awhile, I half-convinced myself that you understood, that you did know, and that my little surprise this weekend wouldn't be much of a surprise to you at all. That—I don't know—that you'd be excited for me."

She said flatly, "You lied to me."

Val started to shake her head, then stopped. "I never wanted to. I didn't intend to. But Cici and the other girls told me you'd misinterpreted my texts, that you were expecting something so very different from this weekend…" She had to pause when she saw Kiki wince. She almost reached for her hand, then thought better of it. "I knew then that surprising you would be cruel, and that doing it at Paul and Derrick's event would be beyond rude. It turns out that trying to deceive you was even more cruel. I never intended to lie," she finished, heavily. "But I did, and I'm sorry. That's all I wanted to say. "

Kiki was silent for a moment, sipping her coffee. Then she said, "I was up all night, reading back through our texts. Wondering how I could have convinced myself that..." She let the sentence trail off. "I guess I was just so lonely, and scared, after the divorce. Everything was falling apart, but at least I still had you. And then there was that stupid promise we made about marrying each other if we were still single at fifty." She sighed. "We would have made a great couple."

Val smiled gently. "You bet we would have."

"Last night at dinner," she said, "I said I knew just to save face. I guess you figured that out."

Val nodded. "Everybody thought you'd go ballistic. I'm glad you didn't."

Now it was Kiki's turn to smile, though painfully. "I've changed too. After the divorce, I realized dramatics hardly ever got me what I wanted."

"I like the new you," Val said.

Kiki took another sip of her coffee. "Anyway, I did a lot of thinking last night, a lot of remembering, a lot of putting pieces together. And I realized that, in a way, I *did* know. I think I've known for a long time." She looked at Val, holding her gaze for the first time. "I know," she said. "And it's okay."

A tenuous smile quivered at the corner of Val's lips, and her eyes misted. "Thank you," she said. "That means… everything." Hesitantly, she touched Kiki's hand. Kiki didn't pull away.

Kiki said, "I do love you, Ted. I think I just got 'loving' confused with being *in* love."

Val said, "I love you too, Kiki. That much hasn't changed. Only…" She hesitated, then finished, "Could you do me a favor?"

Kiki looked at her inquiringly.

She said, "Call me Val."

Kiki smiled, then turned her gaze to her coffee cup. "I had fun with you at dinner last night."

"It was so good to be with you again," Val said sincerely. "We should have done it sooner. Much sooner."

Kiki nodded. "You look terrific," she said. "But that shade of lipstick you're wearing is all wrong for your skin tone."

She looked surprised. "Seriously? The girl at the cosmetic counter said it was very on trend."

Kiki waved a dismissing hand. "They always say that. You need to go more coral."

Val said, "I guess I still have a lot to learn."

Kiki smiled at her, hesitantly. "Me too."

They shared a smile for a moment, then Kiki said, "I have a hundred questions. A thousand."

"And I've been dying to tell you all about it," Valerie said, and got to her feet. "We've got a lot of catching up to do. But could we do it somewhere warm?"

She extended her hand to Kiki, and without another moment's hesitation, Kiki took it. Arm in arm, the two women walked back to the Hummingbird House.

~11~

"Oh," Derrick said, sinking slowly into chair. "That certainly makes more sense." But his expression as he watched the young man cross the room to pour himself a cup of tea was as baffled as ever.

Paul said on a breath, "Oh, please. This really is too much."

"I can't tell you how sorry I am," Leon said. His expression was grave, and the faint accent he previously affected was completely gone. He lowered his eyes to his cup as he absently stirred the tea. "If I'd had any idea her condition would deteriorate this rapidly I never would have accepted your invitation. But I think you'll agree the best thing for us to do is to spare you—and, frankly, my grandmother—further embarrassment and leave before breakfast."

Derrick began a protest, but Paul interrupted, "Perhaps you wouldn't mind telling us more about your, er, grandmother's condition."

Leon sighed. "Of course not. We owe you at least that much."

Paul gestured him into the chair beside the fireplace, and took his own seat next to Derrick. Leon sat, his cup held between his splayed knees, and took a moment to gather his thoughts. He began, "Several years ago we began to notice that Grams was having trouble with her memory, growing more and more confused… sometimes even believing she was a character in one of her own books, or that other people were."

Derrick made a soft sound of sympathy and placed a hand over his heart. Leon nodded and admitted, "It was difficult to watch. But then she had many perfectly normal days, excellent days, even, and it was easy to pretend she was just fine. But of course she wasn't."

He paused to sip his tea, his eyes bleak. "I am the only grandchild, and my grandmother and I have always been close. After I graduated college, I served as her assistant of sorts, booking engagements, answering mail, even editing her manuscripts. She always called me her 'prince'." He smiled faintly. "Three years ago she went to a fan convention, and she insisted I accompany her dressed as a prince. That was all fine and well, happy to do it, but shortly thereafter she had a stroke, and when she recovered the only memory she held clearly was of our last time together, when I was her prince. Somehow word got out on the fan sites that Esmerelda Delaware had married royalty and, voila, a myth was born."

"Oh," said Derrick softly, eyes watering. "Oh."

"These days," admitted Leon reluctantly, "she really isn't comfortable going out unless I'm with her, playing the role of the prince. It's as though I give her balance, or even—as strange as it sounds—some kind of touchstone to reality. Usually..." He looked at them earnestly. "I swear to you it's true—usually when I'm with her she plays her role to perfection. No one would know there's anything wrong with her mind at all, and if there is a slip or two it's easily attributable to eccentricity. I've never seen her fall apart like this and I'm so desperately sorry. It seems..." He swallowed hard and squared his jaw. "It seems my grandmother's condition has deteriorated to the point that she can no longer manage the stress of travel. I'm afraid there's little hope that she will be able to remain coherent enough to speak in public, or even conduct a question and answer session. I must respectfully ask your understanding, and your forgiveness."

"Well, of course we'll cancel the event," Paul said, his forehead creased with concern. "But please don't feel you have to leave. Perhaps another day or two of rest..."

He shook his head sadly as he stood. "The best thing to do is get her back to her apartment in New York, where everything is familiar. She does much better there."

Derrick's expression was gentled with compassion. "I just don't understand," he said. "Her books are so wonderful, and this last one was nothing short of brilliant. You'd never know anything was wrong."

Leon hesitated, pressing his lips together, and then seemed to come to a decision. "The truth is," he said, "my grandmother hasn't written a book in years."

Derrick smothered a gasp, and Paul said uncertainly, "A ghost writer?"

Leon nodded. "As I mentioned, I've been acting as her assistant for some time now, and I've been her first reader since..." A fond smile touched his lips. "Since I was old enough to read, I suppose. Sometimes I'll help her with research, or plot issues... but when I read the manuscript for *Lost in Love* I was horrified. That was the first book she wrote after her stroke, and while she'd seemed to recover remarkably well for a woman her age—at least that's what the doctors said—something was clearly very wrong. The pages she'd written made no sense at all. The words didn't form sentences. The names of the characters changed on every page. Nothing was as it should have been. Nothing." He took a breath, and the pain of the memory was reflected in his eyes. "Publishers have deadlines, of course, and

Esmerelda Delaware was under contract for eight more books. Her fans were waiting, book tours had been planned. I knew the story she meant to write. We'd been discussing it for months. So I did the only reasonable thing—I wrote the book myself, from start to finish. It did well. Extraordinarily well, actually. No one guessed Esmerelda Delaware hadn't written it herself." He gave a small, deprecating shrug of his shoulders. "And so a grand deception was born. My grandmother sits at her desk for a few minutes each day and scribbles words on a legal pad, and is convinced she's writing a novel. I produce the finished book and no one—not even she—knows the difference."

Derrick regarded him with admiration. "You're really quite good."

And Paul agreed, "You certainly could have your own career. Have you considered branching out on your own?"

He shook his head, smiling. "What I do is a labor of love. Esmerelda Delaware is a legend, and I can't just let her legacy fade into ignominy. Besides..." He shrugged. "I'm really not that talented. I'm just building on what she's already done. And I could never manage celebrity the way she has done. I much prefer to be turning the wheels behind the scene."

Paul said, "I do wish you'd reconsider staying. I'm sure we could work something out about the tea, and it seems such a great shame to have you both miss out on the weekend."

Leon replied, "Thank you. I appreciate your support and your understanding, but I really think it's best if we leave now, before anyone else is up and about."

A sharp voice demanded behind them, "Leave now? Before the tea? Have you lost your mind, child?"

They all turned to find Esmerelda Delaware standing in the doorway, scowling at them. She was fully made up, wearing a long pink satin robe trimmed with white feathers and matching pink satin mules, her hair curled and tied back with a pink satin bow. She went on, mildly outraged, "I certainly hope you're not suggesting that I disappoint my fans. I've never done so before and I have no intention of starting now! I have a perfectly lovely speech to give—which, I might add, I even went to the trouble of memorizing—so you can just get that nonsense about an early departure out of your mind."

She turned from an astonished Leon to an equally astonished Paul. "And now, my good sir, if you would be so kind as to have one of the servants bring breakfast to my room I will be most grateful. I intend to spend the rest of the day there in quiet repose, preparing for my appearance this afternoon. Do please see that I am not disturbed."

She turned with a flutter of feathers and left the room, leaving the three men to stare at one another, stunned and speechless.

~*~

From *The Happy Traveler* Blog
February 14

To take tea at the Hummingbird House is to be transported back to a time in which decency and gentility were the rule, not the exception, in which respect for one another was simply a matter of good manners and good manners, my dears, were a requirement for mixing in polite society. Imagine if you will a room staged with half a dozen round tables covered in pink cloths, set with delicate Havilland in a rose pattern, and white, lace-trimmed napkins. Each table is adorned with a small bouquet of red roses in a crystal vase, and a tall silver serving tree offering a variety of sweet breads and tea sandwiches. The air is lightly scented by lilac candles and the murmur of gentle conversation blends with the classical music playing softly in the background. The first course is a lovely minted pea soup, followed by a Chesapeake Bay crab quiche served piping hot. Your hosts move from table to table, pouring tea from silver pots, insuring your comfort and making pleasant, never intrusive, conversation. If you are fortunate, you are looking into the eyes of someone whose companionship you value above all others. This is civilization as it was meant to be. This is tea time at the Hummingbird House.

~12~

"And so," Derrick whispered to Cici, Lindsay and Bridget as he bent to fill their cups, "that's how we left it. She was perfectly fine—except for being a fraud of course—and insisted on making her appearance this afternoon as planned." He cast a nervous glance over his shoulder. "Except that she hasn't quite done that yet, has she?"

"Wait," said Cici, looking baffled. "Esmerelda Delaware didn't even write *Love Lay Dying*?"

"But I brought my book for her to sign!" Bridget protested.

"Shh!" Derrick looked around furtively, alarmed. "It's supposed to be a secret!"

"And the prince isn't even a prince?" Lindsay said. She looked disappointed for a moment, and then shrugged. "Although, come to think of it, he wasn't very convincing."

Again Derrick cautioned, "Shh! Don't make me sorry I confided in you." And he scurried off, making sure to erase the anxiety from his face before he reached the next table.

Paul was next. "If we somehow manage to get through this weekend with our reputation intact," he said distractedly, "we are *never* hosting another event. Is everything all right here? Enjoying your tea?"

Lindsay pointed out, "You make your living hosting events."

Cici said, "Everything's perfect, Paul, just like it always is. Have you talked to Kiki and Val? What happened after we left last night? Do you think they worked things out?" She nodded toward the table where Val sat with another couple at a table for four. The empty place beside her looked forlorn, and Kiki was nowhere to be seen.

"I don't know," he answered unhappily. "I can only hope so. I haven't talked to either of them since before breakfast. To be perfectly honest, I can only deal with one crisis at a time. How was the quiche? Please tell me it was wonderful. I've been too nervous to eat." He glanced at his watch. "Five minutes. If they're not here in five minutes I'm going to knock on her door."

Purline said, "If you're looking for that queen, she's coming down the hallway."

Paul said, "Oh, thank God." He went to meet the latecomers, moving quickly toward the hall.

Purline removed their quiche dishes. "My great granny had the dementia," she said. "Croaked like a frog everywhere she went. Came to supper one night wearing her underpants on her head. Never did know what she was going to do next. You got to watch them every minute, you know. A person has to feel sorry for that prince fellow. It's rough on the loved ones."

"Actually," Bridget said, lowering her voice confidentially, "he's not a prince. He's her grandson."

Purline almost dropped the plates. "She's married to her *grandson*?"

"No, no," Lindsay said quickly while Cici made frantic shushing motions with her hands, glancing around to make sure no one had overheard. "They're not married. Just pretending."

"And no one's supposed to know," added Cici. "So please keep this to yourself."

Purline stared at them. "So let me get this straight. You got a queen that's not a queen, married to a prince that's not a prince, only they're not really married at all, and nobody's supposed to know about it? On top of that you've got a man that's not a man any longer running around like a woman pretending to be somebody else so his girlfriend don't catch on. Sweet Jesus, take me now. I feel like I'm living right smack in the middle of Sodom and Gomorrah. Is anybody in this house who they're suppose to be?"

She turned on her heel and strode away, pony tail bouncing. The three women looked at each other uncomfortably.

"Oh, Lord," Derrick said under his breath, standing beside them again with an empty teapot in his hand. "She's right. We brought this all on ourselves. Secrets and lies and deception… they never end up in anything but a mess. Just one big, tragic mess."

Bridget said, starting to stand, "Well, we can't do anything about Esmerelda Delaware and her royal ghostwriter, but I'm going to go talk to Val. The whole thing with Kiki is partly our fault, you know, and someone needs to apologize to her."

Derrick took a breath and held up a staying hand. "Yes," he agreed, "and that someone needs to be me." He looked at them apologetically. "I should have said something earlier, when I was going around with the tea, and I wanted to. But you know how I get when I'm nervous, all I could talk about was the food. And one hates to intrude in a public setting…"

Cici pushed back her chair. "I don't," she said, crumpling up her napkin. "We'll all go."

They made their way around the tables to the one where Valerie was sitting with the couple from Michigan, apparently in the middle of a story about something that had to do with the Swiss Alps. Derrick lay a hand upon the back of her chair and said gently,

"I'm so sorry to interrupt. I just wanted to make sure everything was okay here. Did you like the quiche? It's from a recipe we found in *Southern Living*. We were nervous about it at first, but Purline does an excellent job at copying recipes and…"

"Valerie," Cici interrupted firmly, smiling her apologies at the puzzled-looking couple across the table, "we were hoping to talk to you for a minute."

Val regarded them with a curious smile.

"We just wanted to apologize for last night," Bridget added in a near-whisper.

"We felt so bad about everything," said Lindsay.

"All of us," Derrick said quickly. "All of us felt bad."

"We just wanted to say," Cici began, but before she could finish her sentence, Kiki edged in between them, flushed and breathless as she slid into her seat at the table.

"I'm so sorry!" she exclaimed. Then, glancing at the small surprised crowd standing around the table, she added, "Hi, everyone. I'm sorry to be late, but I had to go all the way to Stanton for this."

She pulled a rectangular gift-wrapped package from her purse and presented it with a flourish to Valerie. Valerie's eyes sparkled with excitement as she slit the tape with a fingernail. The others shared a look of puzzlement.

"Chocolates?" Valerie guessed, and then laughed with delight as the paper fell away. "It's Esmerelda Delaware's book!" she exclaimed. "*Love Lay Dying!*"

"You said last night you'd forgotten your copy," Kiki explained, "and you simply *have* to get it signed. Who knows when you'll have another chance?"

Valerie leaned across the place setting and hugged Kiki with one arm. "You are the sweetest thing! Thank you!"

"I got chocolates, too," Kiki assured her, grinning. "We'll break into them later."

Lindsay said uncertainly, "So... I guess everything is all right here."

"Except that I'm starving," said Kiki, reaching for a tea sandwich from the tiered server. "Hi, I'm Kiki," she said to the couple across the table, extending her hand. "Val and I have known each other forever."

"Well now, isn't that wonderful?" Derrick murmured while introductions were made. He looked relieved that the drama was resolved, but also a little disappointed that he had played no part in resolving it.

"Lots to tell you all," Val said. Her smile was warm and relaxed as she looked up at them. "Let's get together after..."

She was interrupted by the clinking of a spoon against a glass, and they all turned to see Paul standing at the front of the room. A small lectern had been brought in, and on either side of it sat the guests of honor: Esmerelda Delaware, in a print dress and be-flowered tea hat, and her escort Leon, who had abandoned his uniform today for a snappy blue blazer, ascot, and khakis.

"Ladies and gentlemen," Paul said, tapping the spoon against the glass again. "Ladies and gentlemen, your attention please. If you'll all take your seats..." He looked purposefully at Cici, Lindsay and Bridget, who quickly tiptoed back to their table. "It's my very great pleasure to formally introduce to you our guest speaker, Miss Esmerelda Delaware, author of so many of our favorite romantic novels, most recently, *Love Lay*

Dying. Miss Delaware has prepared a few remarks for you, after which we will open the floor for questions. My friends and valued guests, I give you the Queen of Romance, Esmerelda Delaware."

The fact that Paul, who loved little more than the sound of his own voice and who could extemporize a twenty-minute speech on two seconds' notice, had kept his introduction deliberately short was a dead giveaway to his anxiety. He led the applause and retreated to stand beside the door as Esmerelda Delaware got to her feet and approached the lectern. Only then did he take a handkerchief from his breast pocket and dab discreetly at his forehead.

Esmerelda Delaware folded her hands atop the lectern and surveyed the crowd with a regal gaze. "My lords and ladies," she began, generating a few giggles from the crowd as everyone settled back with expectant smiles, "thank you for inviting me to address you today. Four score and seven years ago our forefathers brought forth upon this nation a great plague, in which it rained for forty days and forty nights, which happens to be precisely the number of books I've written. Or is it forty-three? One really can't be expected to remember such details, now can one? Particularly when taking into account the three blind mice. But of this I can assure you, my dears, the secret to a long and healthy life is a double shot of whiskey and an afternoon nap." She smiled benignly. "Are there any questions?"

The alarm that had crept into Paul's eyes when she first began to speak had now turned to panic, while the looks that her listeners shared ranged from confusion to amusement. A hand shot up, and a woman stood, pressing a copy of *Love Lay Dying* against her chest like a talisman. "Miss Delaware, it's such a pleasure to be able to talk to you in person. I love all your books, but *Love Lay Dying* is my favorite. Please tell me this isn't the last one in the series!"

"Very well," replied Esmerelda Delaware. "I won't." She looked around the room. "Other questions?"

The woman looked around uncertainly, gave a wavering smile, and then sat down.

Paul tried, and failed, to look casual as he crossed the room and knelt beside Leon's chair. His smile was frozen in place, his eyes frantic. He whispered, "You've got to do something!"

"What?" the erstwhile prince whispered back, looking equally as frantic. "What would you have me do?"

From the back of the room another woman stood. Paul smothered a groan.

"Miss Delaware," she said crisply, "I'm Marcie Williams from the Stanton *Chronicle,* and our readers would love to know how you came up with the character of Elana St. Vincent. Also, don't you think, in this era of women's empowerment, she represents—well, to be perfectly frank—all that is wrong with this world?"

Paul froze, his eyes meeting those of a desperate Derrick across the room. He could feel Leon stiffen beside him. All eyes were turned attentively toward Esmerelda, who, after a single agonizing moment, gave a light dismissive laugh. "How the bloody hell should I know? I haven't even read the thing. Thank you all for coming. Please make sure your seats and tray tables are in an upright position, and enjoy your flight. Good day."

And with that, she left the lectern and took her seat next to it, still smiling regally.

Paul whispered desperately, "Listen to me. You said you couldn't let your grandmother's legacy die in ignominy. Don't you see that's exactly what's going to happen if you don't say something? She'll be remembered as a joke!"

The reporter said sharply, "Excuse me, Miss Delaware? Could you explain that, please? I asked a serious question."

Leon's jaw tightened. "I don't know what you expect me to do."

The members of the audience shuffled in their seats, murmuring to each other and looking uneasy. Esmerelda Delaware regarded them all serenely, and said nothing.

Paul placed a hand on the other man's shoulder, tightening his fingers. "These people adore your grandmother," he said. "Her words mean something to them. Tell them the truth. They deserve that. And..." He drew a breath. "...take it from someone who knows. No good ever comes from anything less."

Leon regarded him steadily for another moment, then abruptly got to his feet. He straightened his jacket, walked to the lectern, and looked out over the room.

"I am Leon Frederickson," he said. "And as many of you may have surmised by now, I am not a prince. I only play one on occasions like this." He gave a wan smile that coaxed a chuckle out of some of the onlookers. Encouraged, he went on, "I am, in fact, a very proud grandson who is more than pleased to support my grandmother in whatever role she assigns to me."

This caused a few ripples of surprise to go through the audience, and the reporter sat down, holding her phone straight out with one hand to record his words while scribbling busily on the notepad in her lap with the other hand.

"My grandmother," Leon said, "the great Esmerelda Delaware, is in the business of spinning dreams, and in these harsh times I cannot think of a more noble endeavor. There are those who might call her stories silly and her characters vapid. But I have had the great privilege over the past several years of helping to weave those stories, and bring those characters to life. And I can assure you, there is nothing vapid or silly about the quest for love. It is at the heart of what makes us human. So to answer your question, Miss Williams, I believe that Elana St.Vincent is one of the most empowered females in literature. She fought armies, crossed oceans, endured savage mistreatment, and outwitted captors for the sake of the one she loved. Can there be anything more heroic? Upon the hearts of such women civilizations are built."

He sought out the woman who had asked the first question, and smiled at her. "You asked about the end of the series. My grandmother has created characters with destinies of their own and stories so vivid they will live forever." He looked at his grandmother with sorrow in his eyes, and she smiled back at him benignly. He turned back to the audience. "It is a sad but true fact of life that the creators often lack the stamina of their creations, and over the past years my grandmother's increasing frailty has caused her to reach out to me for assistance. I have grown accustomed to picking up the pen when hers faltered, and I will continue to do so for as long as I am needed. I vow to you now, as long as you continue to ask for the stories, they will continue to be written."

The audience erupted into a clatter of excited questions and Paul felt his shoulders sag with relief. He slipped out into the hallway, once again reaching for his handkerchief to mop his brow. Derrick joined him a moment later.

"Well," Derrick said, fanning himself with his hand, "we managed to scrape by on that one. How, I'll never know. And no one seems to be at all upset that Leon wrote the last few books. They think it's delightfully naughty."

"Lesson learned," Paul said, heaving a huge sigh. "If ever again there's any doubt, honesty is definitely the best policy. Is it five o'clock yet? I need a drink."

"I feel a little sorry for Miss Delaware though," Derrick said. "The poor thing doesn't have a clue."

Behind them, Esmerelda Delaware chuckled. "I wouldn't exactly say that."

They both whirled. "Miss Delaware! We didn't see you there!"

She responded with a nod toward the room she had just exited. "I'd say it's all coming together rather nicely, wouldn't you? More or less according to plan. And as long as you're pouring, young man, I'll have a Scotch. Never did develop a taste for tea."

Paul and Derrick stared at her. Derrick said carefully, "Plan? There was a plan?"

She smiled at them. "And I do appreciate your help with it, gentlemen, which is why I'm now going to tell you my secret." She glanced over her shoulder again and then back at them, her eyes twinkling. "I am not crazy," she confided. "And I'm not senile. What I am is an eighty-four-year-old woman with a heart condition who has already had one stroke and has no delusions of living forever. My grandson, on the other hand, is an enormously talented boy with absolutely no confidence in his own ability. I've been trying for years to convince him to turn his hand toward writing a novel, but he insisted the only thing he was good for was running the business. But when the chips were down—with six months to deadline and a contract hanging in the balance—I knew he'd come through, and so he did."

"Wait," Paul said uncertainly. "You pretended to write a bad book so that he would have to take over?"

She gave a single self-congratulatory nod. "Brilliant, wasn't it? And it wasn't even that difficult to pull off. I even fooled the doctors. To tell the truth," she added with a grin, "It was all rather a blast, playing make-believe."

Derrick and Paul shared an uncertain, disapproving look. "But," Derrick said, "your grandson is so worried about you."

She gave a careless wave of her hand. "Oh don't worry," she said. "I'm going to make a remarkable recovery the minute we leave here. Leon would have been content to go the rest of his life letting the world believe I was still writing those novels," she added. "I had to find a way to make him stand up and take credit for his work. The best way to do it was in a safe environment like this, among a small group of dedicated readers. Good heavens, why else do you imagine I accepted this engagement?"

Neither Paul nor Derrick had a reply for this. They just stood there, looking stunned and confused, until she gave them each a reassuring pat on the arm.

"The point is," she said, "everything worked out the way it was supposed to. We're making a guest appearance at the Romance Writers of America Conference this summer—huge thing, thousands of people—where we'll make the official announcement that my darling Leon is the secret behind the success of the last three books. I have no doubt he'll be besieged by agents and publishers, and his career will be launched." She paused for a moment, smiling tenderly, and then added pragmatically, "But he'll have to finish out my contract first, of course." She turned back to Paul, her tone brisk. "Now, young man, about that drink?"

Paul blinked, anchoring himself back in reality. "Oh. Yes, of course." He turned toward the dining room.

"And put it in a teacup," she called after him. "I don't want my grandson to know."

~12~

Check out at the Hummingbird House was 11:00 AM. Paul and Derrick stood on the front porch with Harmony, watching the black limousine drive away with Esmerelda Delaware and Leon Frederickson inside. It was all the two men could do not to sag with relief, but Harmony, wrapped in a purple mohair shawl against the February chill, looked extremely pleased with herself.

"What can I tell you, boys?" she said. "The stars don't lie."

"Then they're the only things that don't," Paul muttered.

Derrick said, trying to put a cheerful spin on it, "At least everyone had a good time. And you know what they say. All's well that—"

Paul interrupted darkly, "Don't say it."

A blue sedan pulled up and Kiki came out, dressed for traveling and dragging her roll-on. "That's my Uber," she said. She hugged each of the men in turn. "Thanks, guys. It's been quite a weekend! Great seeing you both. We've got to do this again soon."

They hugged her back and said what they hoped were the proper things but were glad to be interrupted when Val came out. The two women embraced, and Val said, "I wish you'd let me give you a ride to the airport."

"Don't be silly. It's out of your way." She stepped back, smiling, holding her hands. "Take care of yourself. I'll see you in April."

"We're going to Belize," Val told Paul and Derrick. "I've never been."

Kiki added, "And it's the first time I've ever gone with a girlfriend." She grinned and told Val, "I'll text you from the airport."

"Call me," Val corrected firmly. "On the telephone."

She laughed and blew them all a kiss as she went down the steps and got in the car.

Val turned to the two men. "Thank you," she said sincerely, "for your hospitality. I know it probably wasn't exactly what you'd planned, but the weekend meant the world to me."

Paul offered his hand. "I'm just glad things worked out for you. And again, I apologize for anything I did that made things harder for you."

Derrick was less formal, hugging her. "I don't feel like we've had any time to chat!" he said. "You know you're welcome to stay another day or two. We could catch up."

"I'd love to," Val assured him, "but I'm off to New Orleans for Mardi Gras. Work, you know."

Both men looked surprised. "Oh?" Paul said. "I was under the impression you were retired."

And Derrick asked with interest, "What kind of work do you do?"

She smiled and picked up her shoulder bag. "It's more of a hobby, really," she said. "I write a little blog."

Now even Harmony looked surprised. She stepped forward. "A *travel* blog?"

Valerie smiled and waved as she started down the steps. "That's right," she said. "I'll send you a link."

The three of them stood there with smiles frozen in astonishment and waved politely as she drove away.

Then they turned without a word and went back into the house.

~*~

From *The Happy Traveler* Blog

I like to think, dear readers, that the journeys we take in life are a lot like the journey of life. The road is often twisted and full of surprises, and sometimes it's hard to see around the corners. The destination is hardly ever what we expect, but that's a good thing, because most of the time it's even better. If we're lucky we will make new friends and even meet old ones. We'll have grand adventures that make us laugh and even, on occasion, make us cry. But if our hearts are pure and our minds are open we'll never regret a moment of the trip because, in the end, the only thing that matters is that we had the courage to make the journey.

Until next time, friends and readers, I wish you happy travels!

~*~

The Easter Charade

Or

The Importance of Being Earnest

~1~

Springtime had come to the Hummingbird House. Cherry blossoms lined the curved drive like bridesmaids in ruffled pink gowns. Pink and white dogwoods dotted the lawn with random playfulness while azaleas in shades of fuchsia, peach, champagne and cream lined the paths that meandered through the semi-formal gardens. In the background the mountains were decked out in every shade of green imaginable, from palest lime to deepest spruce, while in the foreground the rich lavenders and pinks of the showy redbud trees provided a gay contrast to the lacy fronds of a weeping willow.

Multicolored tulips blossomed in stone-lined beds, fountains splashed and danced with a lively melody, and pale purple wisteria cascaded artfully over the arched garden gate. An abundance of hummingbirds darted and danced from bud to blossom and drank their fill from the colorful glass globe feeders that accented the garden. It was, in all, precisely the setting to which city-dwellers would flock in order to restore their souls with the richness of nature's bounty.

Or so it promised on the Hummingbird House Bed and Breakfast's website.

In the midst of all this splendor sat a long lodge-like structure with a deep wrap-around porch onto which a series of doors opened, each painted in a different bright enamel color. Each door led to an elegantly decorated guest room whose name corresponded to the color of the door. Those names were constantly changing, however, as the B&B's owners could never quite agree on the theme. Last season the rooms had been named for flowers; before that, an artist's palette. This spring, after a winter spent in debate, the theme was birds.

The lawn surrounding the structure was dotted with laurel-twig furniture where guests might sit and chat on a blue-green evening, sipping fine wine and admiring the fairy lights that twinkled in the trees overhead. At each end of the porch, there were two deep wicker swings decorated with plump down cushions that had been imported from Europe, and along one wall was stationed a long, narrow Biedermeier table upon which canapes and sherry were set out at exactly five o'clock on sunny afternoons. Today, in anticipation of its first gala weekend of the season, the Hummingbird House Bed and Breakfast was polished, painted and decorated within an inch of its life. All the windows were flung open and lace curtains fluttered in the breeze. Every garden table was festooned with a vase of fragrant wisteria. A living wreath of spring blossoms hung on the bright red front door. And just behind that front door, disaster was brewing.

"Mice!" cried Derrick, rushing in from the kitchen. He stopped just short of the elegant reception desk, clapped a hand to his heart, and cast a half-horrified, half-dismayed look over his shoulder, as though he couldn't believe the word had actually come out of his mouth—and that others might have heard it. "Harmony!" This time he reduced his shriek to a desperate stage-whisper. "We have mice!"

The Hummingbird House reception foyer was a study in eclectic elegance, from the impressive display of artwork on the gallery wall to the tall antique reception desk that had been rescued from a country estate in Provence. Above the desk was a carved wooden sign that read, *Don't be afraid to show kindness to strangers, for thereby many have entertained angels unaware.* And upon that desk, in a gracious nod to the season, was a single Easter lily potted in a locally-cast pottery urn, and a woven copper basket containing a collection of reproduction Faberge eggs nestled in a bed of moss. In the nook behind the reception desk a woman sat at a more practical work station, scrolling the screen of her computer and chatting on the phone.

She raised a finger for silence and did not look up from the computer. "Absolutely, darling," she was saying into the phone. "Don't you worry about a thing. I have it down right here. Two turtledoves. And just in case you haven't decided on an officiant, I know a perfectly marvelous shaman..."

The distress in Derrick's eyes grew, if possible, even more pronounced at the mention of more unauthorized creatures in his home — not to mention a shaman, who was definitely not on the guest list for the weekend. He drew a quick breath to protest, but at that moment his partner burst out of the office they shared across the hall.

"Mice?" he demanded indignantly. "Did you say mice? Impossible! We have twelve guests arriving for our spring gala weekend, *and* a fiftieth wedding anniversary *with* a vows renewal ceremony and there will be no mice! None!" He swept his gaze around the foyer, outraged. "Where are they?" He looked ready to take them on one by one if need be. "Show me!"

Paul Slater was a tall, silver-haired man whose general elegance and subtle arrogance suggested that he had never even seen a mouse, much less been required to do battle with one. He had been a renowned style columnist and frequent red-carpet fashion critic before retiring to the Shenandoah valley with his partner Derrick Anderson to purchase the Hummingbird House B&B. But retirement, as he would gladly affirm to anyone who asked, was no excuse for slovenliness, and neither was the country. Even at 8:00 in the morning, hours before the first guest was scheduled to check in at 3:00, he was perfectly coiffed and dressed in a tailored Armani suit with oxblood Italian house slippers and, for a touch of his own springtime flair, a loosely tied daffodil colored neck wrap whose trailing ends were artfully tossed over one shoulder.

As the former owner of several prestigious art galleries in Washington DC, Derrick's sense of color and design was impeccable, and in that way he and Paul fit together like two perfectly cut pieces of the same puzzle. But Derrick had embraced the bucolic lifestyle with a good deal more fervor than had Paul, and today sported a striking pair of bright red overalls over a yellow calico shirt and a carefully frayed straw hat—his morning gardening attire—along with the look of alarm that transformed his normally placid demeanor into a portrait of anxiety and dread.

Derrick drew a breath to answer Paul then, apparently pulled to address an even more pressing concern, turned to Harmony. "Turtledoves?" he demanded. His voice grew half an octave higher with distress. "Did you say *turtledoves*? The kind that fly and leave droppings all over the garden statuary?"

Harmony ended her phone call, jotted a note on the pad beside the phone, and calmly rose from the desk. "The kind that sit atop a cake and look adorable, darling," she assured Derrick. "Confectioner's of course, artfully designed, hand painted, and completely edible. Cost to us, $35.00. Cost to the customer, $175.00."

Paul, who was the businessman in the family, raised his eyebrows, impressed. "Oh, well, in that case," he observed, "completely appropriate. Nice touch."

Derrick looked a little unsettled. "It was an easy mistake," he pointed out defensively. "You remember that wedding planner who wanted to release a hundred white doves into our foyer the moment the vows were spoken."

Paul shuddered. "If the Humane Society hadn't stepped in…"

"Not to mention the Health Department," added Derrick.

"Disaster averted, gentlemen, I agree," said Harmony. "Now, where did you see the mouse? I'll call the exterminator."

Harmony Haven was a dramatic looking woman far beyond the first blush of youth who would never be called beautiful, but she commanded every room she entered. In return for a part- time permanent residency in the fuchsia room she served as the Hummingbird House's general manager, masseuse, and unofficial spiritual advisor. Despite the fact that, as the heiress to one of the most successful hotel chains in the world, she was eminently qualified for the position, Paul and Derrick were still not entirely sure how that had arrangement had come to be.

Derrick corrected urgently, "Mice, not mouse. There must be a whole tribe of them! I was up early to collect produce from the garden," he went on. He turned to Paul, reminding him, "You know how limp the lettuce gets if you wait until the sun hits it, and that trick of soaking it in ice water never really works."

Paul made an impatient circular motion with his hand, urging him to speed it up. Derrick, who was not known for his ability to edit a story, ignored him. "It was a beautiful harvest, too." His eyes shone with the delight of the memory. "Carrots the size of campfire logs! Radishes like baseballs! And the lettuces, I can't even tell you! Why, I filled up the biggest basket we have and it didn't even make a dent in the lettuce patch, I kid you not."

Paul interrupted with a small exasperated sigh— but not, as one might expect, to chide Derrick for hyperbole. The Hummingbird House garden was renowned for its extraordinary yield, and both Paul and Harmony knew Derrick was not exaggerating. Instead, Paul said, "Derrick, I told you, no one says that anymore. It makes you sound like an old lady."

Derrick looked at him blankly. "Says what?"

"'I kid you not'," replied Paul. "It's straight out of a 1980s sit com."

Before Derrick could answer, Harmony flung out a bangle-bracelet adorned arm with a jangle that made Paul wince. "The mouse?" she insisted.

She was tall and strongly built, with a jutting bosom and big hands that were bedecked with a careless variety of real and costume jewelry. Today she wore a shimmering violet caftan and an orange chiffon scarf to tie back her shoulder-length Goldilocks curls, along with a striking set of amethyst chandelier earrings. When she used that tone, men rarely ignored her, and Derrick was no exception.

"So," he hurried on, "I put the basket on the porch and went to find my phone to take a picture for our Facebook page. Hashtag Hummingbird House garden, hashtag salad bar, hashtag..."

Paul smothered a small groan. "Twitter, sweetie," he said. "Hashtags are for *Twitter*."

Derrick gave him another brief look, then shrugged. "Whatever. Anyway, I couldn't have been gone five minutes, ten at the most...okay, fifteen, because I did have to watch that video of the baby wolf and the kitten that Jeremiah sent us." He turned to Paul. "Did you see it? It was really adorable."

Paul spread his hands wide and inquired patiently, "Was there a mouse in it?"

This time the look Derrick gave him was closer to a glare, and he turned deliberately back to Harmony. "When I returned to the porch," he reported, "my beautiful basket of produce had been ravaged. *Ravaged*, I tell you. Lettuce was scattered everywhere, shredded to pieces, and a bite had been taken out of one of the radishes! There were teeth marks on the carrots! Teeth marks!"

Harmony frowned. "That sounds like a lot of damage for a little mouse. I'd say a rat is more likely."

Derrick once again slapped his hand against his chest and closed his eyes against the thought.

Paul said through gritted teeth, "We do not have rats. Impossible. No. Rats."

"It's a two-hundred-year-old house, gentlemen," Harmony pointed out practically. "You have to expect to put up with a rodent or two. They were here long before we were."

"'Tweren't no rat," declared Purline, striding in from the kitchen with just enough authority in her tone to put an end to the matter. "And I don't allow mice anywhere near my kitchen, you can bank on that. Racoon, most likely. Maybe a possum." As though to prove her point, she held up a carrot, easily fourteen inches long, with several clearly visible chunks eaten out of the middle. "You show me a rat that can do that kind of damage, and I'll be looking for another job, that much is for sure. I say racoon."

Purline, in pony-tail, tight jeans and a flowered midi-top, was a local girl of indeterminate age who had taken over the cooking and cleaning duties at the Hummingbird House with all the brisk efficiency of a boot camp drill sergeant. If she said there were no mice, there were no mice.

"Well, that's a relief," declared Harmony. "Heaven knows I don't have time to wait around for the exterminator today." She glided out from behind the reception desk, layers of silk and chiffon fluttering. "Boys, don't forget what I told you about seating the Thomases next to the Brubakers at meals.

One is earth and one is water, and what do those two elements make when mixed together?"

"Mud?" suggested Paul.

She pointed a finger at him, beaming, "Precisely!"

"But they're relatives," Paul pointed out, pretending, for the time being, to indulge her logic. "Or at least the sisters are. Surely they've endured more than one holiday dinner seated next to each other."

"Which is absolutely no reason to allow them to ruin the reception. If I had a nickel for every time I'd been seated next to a completely incompatible fire element…"

Paul pulled a pained face. "Honestly, Harmony, I've already redone the seating chart twice. You don't really expect me to…"

"The racoon!" cried Derrick. "Doesn't anyone care that there's a racoon raiding our porch for produce?"

Harmony looked at him for a moment, her plain face briefly pursed with perplexity. "Well, darling," she replied, "I'm sure it's gone by now."

"Oh, sure," agreed Purline with a nod of her head and a snap of her chewing gum. "Wild critters don't like to hang out where folks are."

"I should certainly hope not," asserted Paul, frowning sharply. "We're having a garden reception for over a dozen guests this afternoon and the last thing we need is to have it crashed by woodland creatures." He looked at her speculatively. "Purline, isn't your husband a hunter?"

Derrick looked even more alarmed, but before he could draw a breath for an objection he was distracted by the clatter of footsteps in the hall-way.

"Mama!" A brown haired, freckle-faced little boy of about six burst into sight around the corner. He ran up to Purline and grabbed her leg. "Mama, have you seen…"

"Jacob," Purline scolded him mildly. "You get back in the kitchen and finish shelling them peas like I told you."

"But…"

"Purline," Paul said sternly, "what is that child doing here? We've talked about this. The Hummingbird House does not offer childcare for its employees. There are far too many valuable…"

"Oh, keep your britches on," she interrupted impatiently. "It's just for an hour while Mama's at the dentist."

Derrick looked uneasily from Purline to the child. "Aren't there two of them?"

"Three," corrected Paul. Despite the fact that she barely looked old enough to be out of high shool, Purline was mother to a set of twin boys and an eight-year-old adopted daughter. Paul's disapproving frown deepened. "And why aren't they in school?"

Her expression was filled with weary tolerance. "You ever hear of Easter? It's spring break."

"Didn't they just have a break?" insisted Derrick.

Purline rolled her eyes. "That was Christmas."

"Good heavens," muttered Paul. "It's beyond me how you ever expect these children to get an education if they never actually attend school."

Harmony said blithely, "This sounds like something you all should work out among yourselves. I really must get to town and see a man about some turtledoves."

She paused suddenly, one hand fluttering to her temple, and cocked her head in an attitude of intense listening. "Oh my," she murmured, "the spirits are chatty today."

Behind her back, Purline rolled her eyes until the whites showed. Paul and Derrick exchanged a look while determinedly holding neutral expressions.

"We do have an interesting collection of guests this weekend," Harmony went on. "And some of them are in for quite a surprise."

"No surprises," Paul said firmly, while Derrick looked at her curiously.

"Good surprises or bad surprises?" Derrick inquired.

"Both, I'm afraid," Harmony said. "But then again, good and bad are all a matter of perception, aren't they?"

"Good is good and bad is bad," Purline put in tartly, scowling. She put her hands protectively on her son's shoulders. "And I don't appreciate you talking that away around my children, either."

"Never mind, Purline." Paul's voice was soothing. "It doesn't matter because there aren't going to be any surprises. Are there, Harmony?" The determination in his gaze suggested that he would be holding her personally responsible should that turn out not to be the case.

"I only report the news, I don't make it," she replied airily. "But if I were you, I'd start making preparations."

"For what?" insisted Derrick. Alarm crept back into his face.

"Anything," she replied, and sounded far too happy about it as she lifted one hand over her head and made a graceful twirling motion in the air with her fingers, as though calling down whatever fortune—or misfortune—might be hovering in the ether. "Anything at all." She moved down the hall toward her room in a trail of patchouli, jingling bracelets and swirling colors.

Paul's frowning gaze followed her. "Flood, famine, high winds?" he suggested, "Forrest fires, swarms of bees…"

"Racoons," supplied Derrick heavily.

"The woman is a nut," pronounced Purline flatly. "The smartest thing you can do is not listen to a word she says. You'll sleep better at night, too."

The little boy tugged impatiently on Purline's leg. "Mama," he insisted, "you have to come!"

"In a minute, honey," she replied, and said to Derrick, "Do you want me to pick some more lettuce for the salad or are you gonna do it?"

"I have a dozen centerpieces and candlescapes to arrange," replied Derrick, sounding harried. "Not to mention the nosegays for the guest rooms."

"And we still have to put together the gift baskets," added Paul.

"Did we decide to chill the champagne for the anniversary couple," inquired Derrick, "or include it in the gift basket?"

"Chilled, definitely," said Paul, motioning him toward the office and the adjacent workroom. "But the monogrammed glasses will be included in the gift basket."

Derrick followed him down the hall. "The last time we did that," he reminded him, "the honeymoon couple stole our ice bucket."

Paul waved a dismissing hand. "We charged them for it."

"It was sterling! And an antique!"

When the two men had disappeared into the office, Purline turned to her youngest and said, "All right, then, what is it you wanted Mama for?"

"Earnest!" the little boy's eyes abruptly flooded with tears. "He's lost!"

"Who?" Purline's shapely brows drew together in perplexity, and then her eyes slowly widened. "You don't mean that rabbit? The one you was supposed to be taking care of for your class over the break?"

He nodded vigorously. "Grandma said not to bring him in the house when she dropped me off, so I left him in his cage on the porch and when I went out to feed him just now the door was open and he was gone!" He pulled her toward the kitchen. "Mama, you've got to help me find him!"

Purline looked at the gnawed-up carrot in her hand, and then at her son, and then at the hallway down which her two employers had just gone. "Earnest," she said, her tone a little stunned. "The rabbit." Then she turned the child toward the kitchen, ruffling his hair with a reassuring gesture. "Don't you worry, Jacob, we'll find him." She cast another glance over her shoulder toward the hallway, and added under her breath, "I just hope it's before anybody else does."

~2~

Turtledoves: check
Photographer: check
Boarding pass: check
Husband: no check

Maddie Rockwell put her phone away, glanced around the crowded airport gate, and muttered to herself, "Why am I not surprised?"

Already she was beginning to regret even asking Benton to accompany her this weekend. This was supposed to be about her parents, after all, and their fifty years of wedded bliss, not about her and her messed-up life.

Maddie was forty-two years old, the assistant director of public relations for a major Chicago-based insurance company, and the mother of two fairly well-adjusted children, Lilly, age ten and Parker, seven. Despite thirty unwanted pounds that no diet known to man had yet been able to remedy—and she had tried them all—she was an attractive woman; carefully coiffed, thoughtfully styled. She carried herself with poise and confidence: whether she was conducting a staff meeting or a school fundraiser, she always had a plan, and the plan always worked. The only thing she hadn't been able make work, in fact, was her marriage.

Four months ago, Maddie had discovered her husband Benton making out with a twenty-two- year-old intern at his company's Christmas party. Though he insisted it had never gone further than that—and she thought he was probably telling the truth— it soon became apparent that Benton's stumble was only a symptom of a marriage that had been slowly wasting away for years. They had gone through the motions, of course, because that was what one did. But after four weeks of marriage counseling they both had agreed that the tear in the fabric of their marriage was irreparable... or perhaps they had merely agreed that neither one was willing to put in the effort that would be required to repair it. Mostly to appease the marriage counselor, they began a temporary separation, although each of them knew there was nothing temporary about it.

Maddie orchestrated the details with her usual quiet competence and did it so well that the children barely even noticed a change in their family structure. On alternate weeks, one of them lived with the children in the suburban home they all had once shared, while the other lived in a featureless executive apartment downtown with daily maid service that was convenient for both of them to commute to work. At first Maddie had been ashamed of how much she enjoyed her time alone in that elegant apartment, where the counters were never sticky and there were no sibling squabbles to break up or homework assignments to supervise. But the novelty wore off quickly, and it wasn't long before she found herself staying late at the office when it was her turn to stay in town, dreading going back to the deathly silence and cold formality of that empty apartment.

Maddie and Benton shared two homes, but they never saw each other. They communicated about the kids via text. Come to think of it, it wasn't all that different from the life they'd lived before the separation.

Up until this point, neither of them had had the initiative—or perhaps the time—to formally file for divorce, although they knew it was inevitable. But when Benton had agreed to come with her this weekend, he had sounded so uncomfortable when he added, "There's something I'd like to talk to you about, anyway." Maddie knew it was time. She'd had her lawyer draw up the papers and tucked them into her luggage, waiting for Benton to sign. She was the one who always ended up taking care of the details. She should have done it sooner.

The only problem was that Maddie had not told her parents about their separation, much less their impending divorce. And this weekend hardly seemed like the time to do it.

The first boarding call for their flight was announced. Maddie took out her phone again and impatiently texted, *Where R U?* Her husband had never been on time for anything in his life. His sweet, impulsive nature and careless disregard for schedules had both enchanted and frustrated her throughout their marriage. She used to think his easygoing personality was the perfect compliment to her rigid world view; now it just seemed selfish and irresponsible.

He didn't reply to her text. She hadn't expected him to.

While they were away for the weekend, the kids were staying with Benton's parents at their place in the country. They had horses and a golden retriever, and the children loved visiting them there. It was only a two hour drive out of town, and Benton had promised he'd leave in plenty of time to make their flight. Clearly, he hadn't.

Maddie swung the strap of her leather carry on over her shoulder and got to her feet. Let him find his own way to Virginia. She shouldn't have invited him in the first place.

"Maddie!"

She turned to see her husband edging his way through the crowd, waving his boarding pass at her. His raincoat was wrinkled, his hair was wind-blown and he hadn't shaved. Apparently, he'd overslept.

He trotted up to her, exclaiming, "Boy, that was close! Sorry, I overslept. Got a late start."

She replied calmly, "Did you get the children settled at your folks?"

"Oh, sure." They took their places at the end of the line. "Happy as clams. Dad wanted to tell me all about his fishing trip last week, so it took a little longer than I'd thought."

"You might have mentioned to him that you had a flight to catch."

His tone cooled. "I said I was sorry."

Maddie's lips tightened.

They boarded without saying anything else. Maddie took the aisle seat, as she always did, and dodged Benton's clumsy attempts to stuff his raincoat in the overhead bin on top of his carry-on until finally she got up and did it herself. When they were settled in their seats, Benton took out his phone and started checking e-mails. Maddie did the same, even though she didn't see how much could have happened in the ten minutes since she last had checked. She was wrong.

"Terrific," she muttered, and frantically began tapping out her reply. "The minister just canceled. Broke his hip. That crazy woman at the B&B must've gotten the word before I did, she said something about a shaman… what *is* a shaman, anyway?"

"A person generally believed to have access to the world of good and evil spirits, common among some North American and Asian tribal belief systems," replied Benton automatically, and Maddie stared at him.

Benton's encyclopedic knowledge of obscure subjects had amazed Maddie when they were dating and alternately annoyed and amused her during their marriage. She had forgotten how much she missed that about him, and fought back a nostalgic smile. "You really can't help yourself, can you?" She meant it to sound like a rebuke, but couldn't quite manage it. She had never been able to stay mad at Benton when he was being the adorable nerd.

He shrugged apologetically, and grinned the grin that once had melted her heart. She looked quickly back to her phone.

"Anything I can do?" he asked.

"Damn it, the one thing I thought I had locked down," she muttered, scrolling through her contact list. "The one thing Mom and Dad specifically asked for was the minister who married them to officiate at the renewal ceremony."

"Well," offered Benton, "it was fifty years ago. They're lucky he was still alive."

Maddie turned away from him, covering one ear with her hand while she pressed the phone to the other. "Hello? Hello, yes, this is Maddie Rockwell…

yes that's right. Listen, there's been a problem with the minister. Can you.... no, no, absolutely not, no shaman! What I need is... hello? Are you there? Hello?"

"Damn it." She stabbed the disconnect button and sat back against the seat in frustration. It was just as well, because just then the flight attendant came by, checking tray tables and seat belts and reminding them to turn off cell phones in preparation for departure. "I'll have to text Mom when we get in the air. Damn it, I told her not to worry about a thing. I told her I had it all under control."

The anniversary party and vows renewal ceremony had been Maddie's idea, as most things were, as was the plan to recreate her parents' original wedding and official wedding photo from fifty years ago. It had been every bit as complicated as planning an actual wedding, but Maddie hadn't minded. She and Benton had eloped—the first and last impulsive thing she had ever done—and if she was perfectly honest with herself, she had always regretted not having a formal wedding. Planning this event for her parents had made up for that, in a way.

"You know," Benton said, "it doesn't have to be a licensed officiant. This is just a ceremony. Anyone can do it."

"Oh, for heaven's sake, Benton, you don't get it! They were married on *Easter*! It has to be a real minister!"

"The first time," he pointed out patiently. "The *first* time they were married on Easter. But *this* time it will be the day before Easter, and they're not really getting married at all so anyone can officiate. Your brother Jackson has a nice voice."

She gave him one of the looks she usually reserved for her children when they came close to stepping over a line. "Stop helping," she said distinctly.

She saw his jawline harden, and he turned his gaze toward the window, where it remained until they were airborne.

After a moment she glanced over at him and sighed. "I didn't mean to snap at you. I appreciate you doing this for me."

He smiled a little hesitantly. "Not a problem. I've always liked your folks. And I know how much this means to you." A pause. "I don't guess you told them yet. You know, about us."

She drew another breath. "Mom and Dad are so fond of you, and this seemed like a really bad time to break their hearts."

He smiled, relaxing into his seat. "Do you think their hearts would be broken to lose me?"

She frowned a little. "Probably not as much as they're going to be when they hear about the minister."

He said, "Maybe I should volunteer to officiate then." And before she could object, he said quickly, "Just kidding."

Maddie bit back a caustic reply. They had to spend the entire weekend pretending to be more-or-less happily married, and there was no point in making it any more difficult than it had to be. In a moment she remarked, "You've lost weight."

He looked as though he might say something else, and then changed his mind. He shrugged one shoulder. "Keto."

She grunted dismissingly. "Men always lose weight easier than women."

Silence fell again. "It's a shame about the minister," Benton said. "But didn't you say this B&B specialized in events like this? I'm sure they can come up with someone."

"It had better not be a shaman." She took out her phone again. "Anyway, the whole point of getting everybody together at this place was to try to recreate the original wedding photo—the outdoor garden, the women in those empire-waisted bridesmaids dresses—and the minister who performed the original ceremony was the centerpiece of the whole thing. Mom is going to be so upset. She wanted everything to be just perfect."

He gave her an odd look. "Really?"

She looked at him sharply. "What's that supposed to mean?"

"Just that I got the impression your mother really wasn't all that involved in the planning. Let's face it, Maddie, you've been working on this thing for almost a year and from the beginning it's been pretty obvious that you've been trying to make this into the wedding you never had."

She scowled and turned back to her phone. "Oh, for heaven's sake."

"Who knows?" he added lightly. "If we'd had a big wedding in the first place, instead of eloping, things might have turned out differently with us."

She started to make an automatic retort, then reconsidered. "Oh, I don't know," she admitted in a moment. "Our wedding wasn't all that bad." She paused midway through typing the text to her mother, and she couldn't quite prevent the twitch of a reminiscent smile. "Or it wouldn't have been, if you hadn't gotten lost three times on the way to the wedding chapel."

"Only because that drunk gave me the wrong directions."

"It was two blocks away," she pointed out. "We could see the sign from the corner where you stopped to ask for directions."

He grinned. "Remember that guy with the monkey? No wonder we thought we in the wrong place."

She chuckled. "And then you stopped to pick flowers for my bouquet from the pots by the gate and they turned out to be plastic."

"But you carried them anyway, just like they were real."

"The people who ran the wedding chapel had to know we'd stolen them, but they never said a word."

"Well, how could they? We would've just gone next door to the guy with the monkey."

She laughed, and for a moment it was like old times. It was easy to remember why she had married him, easy to forget...

She scowled abruptly and turned back to her phone. "I need to finish this," she said.

Benton hesitated, then turned back to the window. They didn't speak again for the remainder of the flight.

~3~

"Never fear," declared Paul. "I am more than capable of rising to the occasion. I have several wedding ceremony speeches already prepared. There won't be a dry eye in the house."

He made a final adjustment to the half- century old photograph that was the centerpiece of the dining room tablescape and stepped back to admire his work. It really was a masterpiece. The tables had been pushed together to form one long table covered in a white cloth. Down the center of the table was a living runner composed of velvety green sod woven with daisies, baby's breath and violets. Nestled here and there in the grass were porcelain Easter eggs painted in pastel colors, along with mismatched mason jars filled with fragrant lavender and rosemary. Tiny white battery-operated lights were hidden in the foliage, so that when they were turned on at dinner time the centerpiece would glisten with dancing lights, like a miniaturization of the formal garden outside the windows.

The photograph centerpiece was a copy of their guests of honor's original wedding photograph, which had been sent to them by the eldest daughter, Maddie Rockwell, for reference. The bride wore a big-skirted lace and chiffon strapless gown with elbow-length gloves and a tiara veil that, naturally, trailed the ground. The groom was in a dress blue navy uniform. They posed in what was clearly the garden of a country club or some other formally landscaped venue, in front of a garden arch that was decorated with trailing wisteria and peach ribbons, flanked on either side by enormous urns of peach and white roses. The four bridesmaids wore peach gowns tied with trailing sage ribbons which weren't completely hideous. The sage chiffon picture-frame hats, on the other hand, should have been burned before they ever made it into the milliner's box. The groomsmen wore white tuxedos with cummerbunds and bow ties, two in peach and two in lilac, which made Paul wince with embarrassment every time he looked at the photo. But it was, after all, the seventies. The bride carried a bouquet of peach roses and lilac blossoms; the bridesmaids carried bouquets of daisies and pansies.

Recreating the floral elements alone had already cost the anniversary party a fortune.

Paul said suddenly, "You did double-check to make sure the right sized gown was put in the right guest room closet, didn't you? We certainly don't want any confusion on the morning of the ceremony."

The guests' wedding finery had been custom made, according to Maddie Rockwell, who had coordinated the event, and even the bridal gown had required alteration. All of the garments had arrived, carefully labeled with names and sizes, last week via overnight delivery. Purline and Derrick had spent an afternoon steaming and freshening the garments, and carefully hanging them in the appropriate closets. It was all part of the service at the Hummingbird House.

"Not to worry," Derrick assured him. "Everything looks gorgeous. Well," he admitted, "except for the hats. There's not much to be done about them. But back to the subject at hand," he went on, "I'm sure you'd do a beautiful job with the ceremony. Only…"

"Only you ain't even a preacher," Purline said, plopping down a Haviland salad plate at each place with an audible clink.

Derrick winced and came behind her, straightening the salad pates so that the pattern aligned precisely with the pattern on the dinner plate beneath it. "Purline, please," he insisted, "be careful. If you chip even a single plate the whole set is ruined. Haviland hasn't even made this pattern since 1923."

"Bone china," she informed him, "won't chip. That's why folks pay so much for it. My granny had a set just like this," she added, continuing to shuffle out salad plates like cards at a poker table. "She got it from her granny, who brought it over from the old country, and not a chip amongst them."

"Which is all beside the point," said Derrick, put out. "What I was about to say is that it seems to me we have bigger problems, what with an extremely expensive garden ceremony *and* luncheon planned, and racoons running wild around the place. Has anyone thought of setting traps?"

Purline rattled the dishes. "No need for traps," she said sharply. "I told you, that racoon is history."

Paul frowned. "That reminds me, Purline, what on earth is that animal cage doing on the back porch?"

She replied briefly, "It's a racoon trap."

Derrick look startled and Paul looked annoyed. "Well, put it away somewhere, will you? It's tacky. And the last thing we want is a live racoon clattering about in a trap on our back porch in the middle of a garden party, for heaven's sake. Now, to return to the point at hand, it just so happens that you don't have to be ordained to perform a re-commitment ceremony, or even licensed. For heaven's sake, these people have been legally married for fifty years. I'm sure by now what they really crave is a ceremony filled with class and sophistication, words crafted by a genuine professional..."

"Actually," Derrick put in, "the woman I talked to on the phone, Mrs. Rockwell, was very clear that the officiant should be a licensed and ordained minister."

"Which," announced Harmony broadly, sailing in from the hallway, "it just so happens I am."

She took a tray of champagne flutes— each one tied with sage green and peach ribbons and each holding a single white votive— from the buffet and followed Purline around the table, setting one candle holder at each place.

Purline gave her a quick suspicious glance. "I never heard of a female preacher."

"Oh, I know a number of them," replied Harmony cheerfully. "Unfortunately, none of the ones I called are available this weekend, including that darling shaman I mentioned earlier, who was called away on an emergency cleansing mission at the last moment."

She paused and glanced around, waiting for someone to ask what an emergency cleansing mission was. Everyone's lips remained deliberately clamped shut.

"So, I am happy to step in," Harmony went on, "being properly ordained by both the Church of The Joyful Noise and the World Love Mission. Also," she added, placing the last candle holder, "I have the perfect outfit to wear. Peach and green with touches of vivid lilac, the bride's colors."

Purline gave a loud and disdainful grunt and bustled off to the butler's pantry.

Paul said, making a notable effort to be diplomatic, "That's really quite generous of you, Harmony, but in this case I tend to agree with Purline."

"Well, of course you do, dear." Harmony gave him an encouraging pat on the arm as she paused to survey the results of their efforts with the table. "You are an *artiste* who really shouldn't be bothered with such mundane details. And may I say, you have really outdone yourself with this table."

Before Paul could begin to preen, Derrick pointed out, "The idea for a living table runner was mine."

She beamed at him, "Well, I can see your hand in every inch of it!" She slipped one arm through his and the other through Paul's. Her expression softened as she looked over the scene. "Look how precious they all are in the photograph. Their whole lives ahead of them, with absolutely no idea what lies before them, and yet they march so bravely on. And now, fifty years later, here they are. They not only survived but thrived. And they're doing it all over again, with four beautiful children and their spouses to take the place of the bridesmaids and groomsmen. That really is something to celebrate, gentlemen, and we all are fortunate to be a part of it!"

Paul and Derrick shared a look, and a single thought. Paul cleared his throat, humbled. "Harmony, that was lovely. Perhaps it would be best, after all, if you…"

But Harmony stopped him with a single raised finger, her gaze focused intently for a moment on something they couldn't see. She closed her eyes, brought her finger briefly to her temple, and then smiled. "Good news, boys," she said. "The spirits tell me everything is going to work out this weekend after all. There might be a little drama, but what fun would life be without it, am I right? The important thing is that everything will come together in the end." She looked at Paul, smiling. "I'm sorry, dear, what were you saying?"

Paul's expression soured. "I believe," he replied, "I'll spend some time practicing my wedding ceremony speech as soon as we finish the table."

Purline burst back through the swinging doors with a tray of silverware clattering in her hands. She began to sort and place the silverware with alarming speed. Harmony backed up to avoid being trampled and Derrick raised both hands in a calming gesture.

"Purline, please! We've talked about this!" He moved in quickly to straighten the salad forks, and to arrange the dessert spoons at a straight parallel to the top of the dinner plates. "If you'll position the butter knife three-quarters of an inch from the edge of the plate and two inches exactly from the edge of table, it will give you a reliable measuring point..."

She cut him off with a look that could have stopped a train. "Don't you start with me about your measuring stick or you'll be sorry you did. I've got no time for that nonsense today and neither do you."

She started slapping silverware down again, and Derrick hurried behind her, doing his best to undo the reckless damage.

Paul said, "Calm down, Purline. This isn't the invasion of Normandy, you know." He took a selection of carefully folded lace-trimmed napkins from the buffet and fell into line behind Purline and Derrick, placing each napkin precisely in the center of each plate.

"Some of us have got better things to do than priss and fuss around all day over a table," Purline replied, not slowing down in the least. "And why you think you've got to have your dinner table set at 2:00 in the afternoon is more than I can figure out, anyway."

"The secret to being a good host," Paul explain patiently, "is advance preparation. Leave nothing to the last minute. That has always been the policy of the Hummingbird House."

"The beds are made," added Harmony, "the rooms are assigned, the gift baskets in place..."

"The nosegays distributed," Derrick put in, "Pansies and daisies, just as requested..."

"The cheese is softening, the wine is breathing," Paul said, "and we are, in fact, quite a bit ahead of schedule."

"Oh, yeah?" challenged Purline, dumping another set of knives, forks and spoons in more-or- less the correct position around a place setting. "Then what's that town car doing pulling up in your driveway?"

For a moment Paul and Derrick's eyes locked in disbelief, and then Harmony rushed to the window.

"Gracious," she said, in a tone that did not in the least convey the gravity of the moment. "It looks like our guest of honor is early."

~4~

Claire Swenson got out of the car, clasping her hands with delight as she looked over their surroundings. "Oh, Henry, it's just perfect!" she exclaimed. "Isn't it just perfect?"

Claire was in her seventies, but often was told she looked no older than sixty, which she happily believed. She worked hard to keep herself fit, fashionable and interested in life—as witnessed by the fact that the wedding dress she wore fifty years ago had to be taken in several inches to fit her now. Her thick, shoulder-length silver bob had just enough blond in it to look natural, and, while she was no stranger to Botox, she didn't believe in over-doing it either. She liked the lines around her eyes, and she never tried to hide a less-than-firm neck with scarves. She was a woman who liked herself and, for the most part, her life, and she wanted to make sure everyone knew it.

"We have *the* most amazing children in the world, don't we?" she went on. "I mean, just look at this place!" She swept an expansive hand around the landscape. "Just like a postcard!"

The anniversary celebration, complete with the vows ceremony and the recreation of the original wedding photograph, had been the brainchild of their eldest daughter, Madeleine, but all four children had pooled their resources to cover the cost of the family weekend.

Her husband, Henry, glanced up from tipping the driver with an absent, if indulgent smile. "Perfect," he agreed.

Henry was a dapper gentleman who wore his age, like his neatly-trimmed gray mustache, well. He had never been one hundred percent onboard with the idea of recreating their wedding, and made no secret of the fact that his idea of the perfect place to celebrate their anniversary would have been a five-star Palm Springs resort. But he had been a good sport about it, as he had been about most everything in their fifty years together.

Claire slipped her arm through his and pressed her cheek against his shoulder. "Thank you for doing this for me, Henry."

He smiled and kissed her hair, his eyes softening with devotion. "Sweetheart, even after all these years, I still can't refuse you anything."

She gave him an impish glance. "Except that honeymoon in the south Pacific."

He groaned. "Believe me, I've been to the South Pacific and you're not missing anything. All that humidity. You'd hate it."

"*You*'d hate it," she corrected. "But I have a feeling those topless Polynesian girls would make up for it." Before he could argue, she added, "This place is charming though, isn't it? It reminds me a little of that place we stayed in Greece."

"But without all the steps," he said. "I swear, honey, as cute as you are, I don't know how I let you talk me into staying in a house that you had to climb halfway up a mountain to get to."

She punched him lightly in the arm, pulling a face. "You sound like an old man."

"I *am* an old man."

"Well, try to have fun this weekend, will you? The kids went to an awful lot of trouble."

He patted her hand absently. "Like I said, dear, anything for you."

The driver started up the steps with their luggage just as the front door opened and their hosts emerged, each impeccably dressed and beaming their welcome. "Mr. and Mrs. Swenson," said Paul, extending his hands to greet them. "Welcome! You're the first to arrive."

"We're a little early," replied Claire. "I hope it's okay."

"The traffic was lighter than we expected," explained Henry.

"Not at all, we're delighted to see you," Derrick assured them. "I'm Derrick Anderson and this is my partner, Paul Slater. I believe we've spoken on the phone."

They shook hands all around.

Derrick said, "We were so sorry to hear that your minister had to cancel. But I want to assure you we're working hard to find a suitable substitute, and I promise that your ceremony will be as flawless as we can possibly make it."

Claire waved a dismissing hand. "Oh please, I hardly knew the man. It was all Maddie's idea to have him, anyway. Whoever you come up with will be fine, I'm sure."

Paul and Derrick shared a look that was part triumph, part relief.

"We've been in very close contact with your daughter," Paul said, "and I think you'll find everything to your liking. We'd be happy to go over the menu with you and give you a tour of the facility once you're settled."

"Oh, it's just like I imagined!" exclaimed Claire, her eyes shining. "Even better. Maddie told me about the painted doors, and how each one represents the color scheme of the suite. Which one are we in?"

"You will adore the Goldfinch room," Derrick assured her, gesturing toward the yellow door at the end of the porch. He gave a sharp crook of his finger toward the driver, who still hovered with their luggage. "The yellow door, my good man, the yellow one."

Claire laughed and laid her hand on his arm as they started up the steps. "You are as charming as Maddie said. What a perfectly marvelous idea this was!"

"Your room is on the corner," Derrick assure her, gesturing the way, "with a lovely view of the garden where we've set up for the ceremony tomorrow. You be certain to let us know if there's anything, anything at all, you want to change. This weekend is all about you, and we're here to serve."

"Aren't you just a dear!" declared Claire as they moved toward the corner room with the yellow door.

Henry held back, and when Paul gestured him to precede him up the steps he said, "Listen, old man, I wonder if you'd do me favor."

Paul looked at him inquiringly.

Henry looked a little abashed as he said, "I know this is really last-minute, and hell, we're both to old for this kind of thing anyway, but..." He reached into his pocket and took out an envelope. "The one thing Claire has always wanted was a vacation in the south Pacific. Couldn't afford it for our honeymoon, and there's always been something over the years that kept us from getting there, but now…" He opened the envelope and took out an embossed folder. He opened it to reveal a brochure depicting gorgeous white beaches and turquoise water, along with two glossy black tickets with "Round Trip" embossed in gold on each one.

"I booked a trip to Fiji tomorrow night. Not exactly my cup of tea, but there's a championship golf course at the resort there so I thought, Why not? I had a buddy of mine print up these fancy tickets and thought I'd wrap them up somehow and surprise her, but I'm no good at that kind of thing. I was wondering if you could do something corny like, I don't know, hide the tickets in the wedding cake or— no, that wouldn't work, they'd get all mushy—maybe serve them to her with dessert at lunch tomorrow somehow… you probably have better ideas than I do, you do this kind of thing all the time. "

He thrust the folder at Paul, and Paul took them, smiling. Nothing in his eyes revealed any doubt whatsoever about being able to fulfill his guest's request. "Well," he said. "Well, of course! Our pleasure. You just leave it to me. We'll think of something absolutely perfect. Don't worry about a thing."

The other man relaxed and gave a decisive nod. "Excellent. So, the yellow room, you say?"

When the guests of honor were settled in their room, sipping champagne and marveling over the details of the weekend the Hummingbird House had in store for them, Derrick bustled down the hall, an envelope clutched to his chest and a secretive expression on his face.

"You won't believe it," he declared to Paul, who was frowning over his own envelope at the reception desk. "The sweetest thing!' he glanced guiltily over his shoulder and lowered his voice. "The absolutely sweetest thing," he repeated. "Mrs. Swenson got wind of the fact that her husband was feeling sad because he'd given up their vacation to Palm Springs for this weekend, so look!" He took two glossy card-stock tickets out of the envelope and presented them with a flourish. Each was embellished with a color collage of a golf course and had the words "Guest Pass" printed on top. "She booked them two weeks at a Palm Springs resort as a surprise second honeymoon! She had the hotel print these out so she'd have something to give him at their anniversary luncheon tomorrow. She wants us to wrap them up and place them on his plate. Isn't that the *most* divine thing?"

Paul took the tickets and looked at them blankly for a moment. "Divine," he agreed, and passed his own set of tickets across the desk to Derrick. "It would appear both members of our charming couple had the same idea."

Derrick looked at two sets of tickets, and then at Paul, his eyebrows raised. "Oh my," he said.

And Paul agreed, "To say the least."

~5~

Claire and Henry Swenson had raised three fine daughters and one son, all of whom had gone on to have careers in the professions or in academia, and all of whom had married perfectly lovely spouses. They flew in from Texas, Seattle, and California to celebrate the event that had been a year in the planning, and they joked that they only did it because they were too afraid of Maddie to refuse. They did it to honor their parents, whose lives had been a model of perfection for them. Also, because no one wanted to cross Maddie.

Excepting the anniversary couple's early arrival, the family members arrived precisely as scheduled. The couples were settled in their assigned suites— The Bluebird, the Cardinal, and the Parrot— where gift baskets and vases of lilacs awaited them, along with a small gold box of Belgium chocolates and a nosegay of fresh pansies and daisies thoughtfully placed in the center of each bed. Paul greeted new arrivals and escorted them to their suites while Derrick served specialty cocktails in the garden. The sound of laughter and excited greetings from reunited family members danced on the spring breeze that wafted through the corridors of the house.

Benton and Madeleine Rockwell were the last to arrive. Paul found Maddie to be exactly as she had sounded on the phone: brisk, decisive and no-nonsense. She was auburn-haired and statuesque, wearing a pale green Chanel suit and a black silk blouse with three-inch heels. Paul had to admire a woman who would tolerate that amount of discomfort on a cross-country flight just for the sake of looking stylish. Her husband, on the other hand, was easy-going and rumpled, dressed in jeans and sneakers and carrying a leather duffle over his shoulder. Paul seemed to recall that he worked in the tech field, which made sense. Benton moved at an easy, ambling pace, stopping to admire the art in the reception area and the mountain view from the front garden, while his wife never even looked up from her phone.

"We've put you in the Hummingbird Suite," Paul said. He opened the emerald door with a flourish and ushered Benton and Maddie Rockwell inside. "It's one of my favorites. I love the view of the mountains from the west, and at night you can hear the splashing of the fountain if you leave the windows open. So soothing."

Benton went over to the open window and braced his hands upon the sill, looking out. "Nice," he said. "Smell that country air."

Maddie looked up from her phone long enough to remark, "Yes. Quite nice."

Paul went on, "All of the wedding attire arrived from the seamstress as scheduled and has been distributed to the appropriate guest's room. The florist will be here first thing in the morning with the bouquets and the floral accents, and we've engaged a harpist as you requested. The weather forecast is for sunny skies and temperatures in the seventies, perfect for a garden party. Wouldn't you agree?"

Maddie replied absently, "Hmm. Perfect."

Paul went on, "As soon as you get settled, please join us on the back terrace for cocktails. The rest of the family is already there. Dinner will be at seven, and the spa is open until 9:00 p.m. If you've booked a massage, your appointment time is confirmed on the card beside your gift basket. Breakfast will be served from 8:00 until 9:30 in the morning and the ceremony will be at 1:00 p.m., as requested, followed by luncheon in the garden. Now, regarding the officiant, I had a thought and I just need you to sign off on it. Since this isn't a legal ceremony, and you don't necessarily need an ordained minister..."

Benton turned from the window, smiling. "Told you."

"Oh, for heaven's sake, don't start in on me again about Jackson." She put her phone away with a final, brief scowl at the contents of the screen she had been reading and explained to Paul, "Jackson is my brother. You can't miss him. He's the biggest loudmouth in the group, and that's his *only* qualification. Besides, I need him to take the place of one of the groomsmen for the photograph, and I must have a minister for the ceremony. It's *Easter*, for heaven's sake."

"Well, technically," Paul began.

Maddie interrupted, "Surely you can find someone to step in. Aren't there any churches around here?"

"We have in fact contacted several clergymen in the area," Paul assured her, "as well as our customary list of officiants who specialize in events like this. Unfortunately, no one is available on such short notice, however, as I was about to explain, I have a suggestion...."

It was at that moment that Paul's gaze happened to fall upon the tastefully dressed and carefully made bed and froze there for half a second of shock. All that remained of the pansy-and-daisy nosegay that Derrick had so meticulously crafted was a pile of petals and shredded jute in the center of the bed. Paul stepped forward on the pretense of fluffing the pillows, swept the remnants of the nosegay into his pocket, and continued without missing a beat, "…that I'd love to discuss with you over a drink in the garden. Just follow the porch all the way around to the back when you're ready."

Still smiling genially, Paul left the room and closed the door with a quick quiet snap behind him.

He walked with a long, determined stride through the common area, past the kitchen where Purline was still banging pots and pans around—and creating mouth-watering aromas in the process—and out onto the back terrace. He kept a smile at the ready and one hand his jacket pocket, fiercely wound around the remnants of nosegay. Derrick was mixing peach Bellinis with organic geranium blossoms at the drink station by the French doors and beaming beneficently over the scene. The wedding arch had already been decorated with wisteria in the center of the garden, and small tables were set at random near the flower beds and along the paths. The central fountain splashed musically, and the meticulously manicured lawn practically gleamed with care. Urns of pansies in the richest of hues flanked the stone pathways, along which couples mingled and chatted and sipped their drinks.

"It's really going quite well," Derrick informed Paul. He gave the Bellini a final stir, topped it with a carefully chosen blossom, and handed the glass to Paul. "Everyone is remarking how closely our set-up resembles the original portrait, and we did do quite well, if I do say so. Of course," he added, lowering his voice and leaning in confidentially, "I do have my doubts about how some of these women are going to look in those peach gowns, not to mention the hats." He shuddered elaborately. "But it's an interesting group, and everyone seems to get along beautifully, despite what Harmony said about fire and water, or whatever it was. Now, you see the petite blonde? That's Ashley Stevenson, she wrote a whole series of books on early childhood education, but you'd never know it to talk to her. And her husband, that's the distinguished-looking gentleman in the golf sweater, he..."

"Where is Harmony?" Paul spoke through gritted teeth, his lips frozen into a smile as he nodded and lifted his glass to guests when they caught his eye.

Derrick gave him an arch look at the interruption. "She's giving a massage," he replied. "She's booked until dinnertime. Why?"

Paul withdrew his fist from his pocket and opened his hand to reveal the crushed and shredded petals. "Mice!" he hissed. "We have mice!"

~6~

Benton dropped his duffle on the emerald velvet bench at the foot of the bed and looked at Maddie. "So," he said, smiling a little. "One bed."

She frowned. "Oh, please. We've been married fifteen years. Do you think you could act like a grown up for one weekend? Of course there's only one bed. It's a bed and breakfast, for heaven's sake."

His smile faded. "Right." He went over to the dresser and began to empty his pockets. Phone, keys, wallet. "I'm going to take a shower before dinner."

"I'll check in on the kids." She hesitated before dialing the number and looked over at him. "Benton, we should try to find some time to talk this weekend. You know, about the divorce. We might not get another chance without the kids around."

He stared at her. "Divorce?"

She was annoyed by his surprise, and it showed in her voice. "Well, what did you think, for heaven's sake? We can't go on living like this forever. We need to get on with our lives." She put her phone on the dresser and went over to her bag, unzipping it. The legal sized folder with the divorce documents was on top. "I had my lawyer draw up a draft of the settlement terms. There shouldn't be any problems, we've already talked about most of it. But you should look these over and let me know if there's anything you want to change."

She held out the folder to him, but he did not reach to take it. "The same old Maddie," he murmured. "Always in charge."

"Someone has to be," she returned sharply, and immediately regretted it. But because she was not good at showing regret she just clamped her lips shut and looked away.

He took the folder from her. He looked down at it sadly. "You still blame me, don't you?"

"Who else should I blame?" She tried not to sound angry, which was, in her opinion, a useless and exhausting emotion. She was simply stating facts. "You're the one who had an affair."

"I didn't have an affair," he reminded her gently. He put the folder on the bed. "I'll look this over after dinner. I'm sure it's fine."

He started toward the bathroom, then looked back at her. "Just so you know," he said, "I never wanted Sandra." He sounded tired as he added, "I just wanted your attention."

Maddie had absolutely no reply for that. She stood there, looking at the place he had been, until she heard the shower running. And then she picked up her phone and left the room.

Maddie hadn't been paying attention when her host had given directions, so instead of exiting through the door that led to the wrap-around porch, she went back out into the hall, through the reception foyer, and toward the back of the house, where she could hear the sounds of her family gathered on the terrace. She was just outside the open doors to the dining room when her phone rang. She winced as she remembered she had forgotten to call the children as she'd intended, and she answered the phone, "Maddie Rockwell."

"Oh, Mrs. Rockwell." The woman on the other end sounded surprised. "I thought I'd dialed your husband's phone." But before Maddie could answer the woman went on, "This is Linda from Dr. Hillsman's office. I'm glad I caught you. I've been trying all afternoon and we're about to leave for the weekend. The doctor wanted to let your husband know that we've received the results of his tests, and he'd like you both to come in Monday morning to discuss them. Is 9:00 okay?"

Maddie stopped walking. She held the phone out to look at it and saw that she had, in fact, accidentally grabbed Benton's phone instead of her own. She blinked, trying to orient herself, and then said, "I'm sorry, what did you say? Something about tests?"

"Yes ma'am. We were waiting for the results of the biopsy, but all the lab work is back now so we can schedule a consultation. Dr. Hillsman doesn't like to do this over the phone, I'm sure you understand. So, 9:00 a.m. Monday?"

Again, Maddie blinked. "Um, yes, I guess so. But…"

"Perfect. I have you down for then. Thank you, Mrs. Rockwell. Have a good weekend."

And she was gone.

"Maddie, darling!" Maddie's mother came up behind her and swept her into an embrace, laughing and rocking her in a quick, joyful dance. "Oh, sweetie, have you seen this place? It's perfect, just perfect!"

Maddie hugged her mother back and murmured something—she wasn't entirely sure what—and Claire laughed her infectious laugh and held onto Maddie for another moment.

"Just look at you!" Claire stepped back and held Maddie at arm's length, her eyes dancing. "How do you get more beautiful every year?" She hugged her again, and then slipped her arm through Maddie's. "Have you seen your father? Where's Benton? They're probably off together somewhere talking about heaven knows what. And listen." She lowered her voice confidentially. "Don't you let your father's talk about 'all this silliness', as he puts it, make you think he doesn't appreciate what you've done. He's just as proud of you as he can be."

Her eyes twinkled as she glanced at Maddie. "Besides," she said, "he's going to be in a much better mood tomorrow, when he sees what I got him for our anniversary. A trip to Palm Springs!" Of course," she admitted, "if I'm being honest, I only did it because the hotel happens to be the home of one of the most luxurious spas in the country, so I won't exactly be suffering the whole time he's playing golf. Come and get a drink. This is just the most magical place. Wait until you see what they've done with the garden! It's almost an exact replica of the garden at the country club where we got married, although..." She leaned in closer, squeezing her daughter's arm. "Honestly, I think this one is much prettier. And the hummingbirds! They're everywhere. And, oh, just look what they've done with the dining table!"

She went through the open French doors into the dining room, just as Paul and Derrick were coming in from the terrace through the doors at the opposite end of the room. Both men had strained expressions, which were immediately replaced with broad smiles when they saw their guests. "Ladies," Derrick greeted them warmly. "I see you found each other. Is everything going well? Do you need anything?"

"We were just admiring how beautifully you've put everything together," said Claire, squeezing Maddie's arm again.

"Yes," Maddie said, turning her attention to them with an effort. "Very nice. Really."

"The only thing I wanted to mention," Claire went on, "is that, if it's at all possible, don't seat my daughters Violet and Ashley together. Or their husbands, for that matter."

Paul looked blank, and Derrick provided, sotto voce, "The Thomases and the Brubakers." Paul nodded his enlightenment.

"Separately, they're all delightful," Claire confided. "But put them together and something just happens. They're as dull as mud. Darling!" she exclaimed to Maddie, pressing her hand together at her lips. "Look at the photograph! Oh, my, what memories that brings back! But those hats! What was I thinking?"

"You looked beautiful, Mom," Maddie replied automatically.

The other woman laughed. "Well, I look fifty years younger, that's for sure. I can't believe how fat I was, but that was the fashion back then."

Maddie said, "You probably wore the same size then as I do now."

Her mother looked briefly chagrined. "Oh, honey, I didn't mean…"

Paul said quickly, "Have you had a chance to look at the menu for this evening? We thought we'd start with a fresh asparagus soup…"

"Followed by a simply gorgeous spinach and strawberry salad with gorgonzola and walnuts," added Derrick.

"The spinach is fresh from our garden," Paul put in, "and the strawberries from the farm next door."

"And locally sourced wild-caught trout," Derrick went on, "lightly seared in butter and served with…"

"It sounds lovely," Maddie interjected quickly, cutting him off. "Really, I'm sure it will be fine."

Claire said, "I just love what you've done with the table. Look, Maddie, it's real grass, and the wildflowers are utterly enchanting. How precious, there's even a bunny!"

Paul, who had stepped forward to straighten one of the wine glasses, gave an absent smile of gratitude for the compliment while Derrick said, "What?" It was at that moment that Purline came through the swinging doors with a tray filled with bowls of soup.

Paul said, "Purline, it's much too early to bring in the soup! It must be served ice-cold or…"

He broke off as his eyes fell upon the small, furry, big-eared creature frozen like a stuffed animal in the center of the grassy table-runner, surrounded by violets and pansies. Derrick saw it at the same time and caught his breath. "Oh my God, is that a…"

The rabbit sprang from the table straight toward Purline. The tray flew into the air. The two women squealed and leapt away from the rain of asparagus soup. Purline cried, "Earnest!" and watched as the bunny scampered around the corner, through the French doors, and down the hallway.

Derrick and Paul locked eyes in stunned disbelief, and Derrick finished his sentence matter- of- factly: "Rabbit."

~7~

"Oh, keep your teeth in," Purline said, scrubbing hard with a damp dishtowel at the asparagus stains on the silk wallpaper. "It'll all come out with peroxide and a little white vinegar."

"Not everything can be fixed with hydrogen peroxide and vinegar," replied Paul, exasperated. "And besides, that's hardly the point! The point is…"

"Well, Mrs. Swenson thought the whole thing was adorable," reported Derrick, coming in from the terrace. He closed the door on the sound of laughter and chatter from the garden. "She's telling her children all about it. I made her second drink extra strong. Mrs. Rockwell didn't seem very amused though. She went back to her room." He rubbed his hands together nervously and look from Purline to Derrick. "Seriously, this has got to be some kind of health code violation. What are we going to do about dinner? No sign of the villain, I suppose."

"Don't worry, we'll just follow the sound of the screams," Paul replied grimly. "He'll turn up. Or better yet, escape into the garden where he belongs."

"He'd better not," Purline said, alarmed. "That there's a tame rabbit and he'd be owl bait in no time flat! And I'm not going to spend my hard-earned pay on buying Jacob's class another pet rabbit, I can tell you that much."

"So, tell me again how the class rabbit came to be running—I mean, hopping—loose in the Hummingbird House on our gala spring opening weekend," Derrick said, still looking confused. "I assume this is after he ate his fill of my garden vegetables this morning?"

Purline scrubbed harder at the now barely visible stain on the wallpaper. "Well, you're all the time leaving the back door open, aren't you? Jacob left that rabbit on the porch and I guess he must've gotten out of his cage somehow. With that big basket of food right there by the door he must've just helped himself and come on inside. Anyhow, what matters is we got to get him back."

"I looked everywhere I can think of," Paul said, but the uneasiness in his voice suggested he was more relieved than distressed not to have found the creature. "We can hardly search the guests' rooms while they're here."

"Maybe you can't," replied Purline, "but I got to do turn-down, don't I?"

Both men stared at her. "You never do turn-down!" Derrick said.

Paul stepped forward and took the dish towel from her. "Just leave it, Purline. You're going to wear a hole in the wallpaper. And I forbid you to search our guests' rooms, rabbit or no rabbit. We'll find the vile rodent ourselves."

"He ain't a rodent, he's a—"

"Pet," supplied Derrick, "yes, we know." He glanced anxiously at his watch. "Twenty minutes until dinner," he said. "What are we going to do about the soup course?"

"I got some of that fancy cold potato soup you all like so much in the fridge," Purline said. "I can bring that out."

"Vichyssoise," corrected Paul. "And that was supposed to be for the reception luncheon tomorrow."

"We have plenty of asparagus in the garden," Derrick pointed out. "We could serve asparagus soup tomorrow and the vichyssoise tonight."

Paul gave a curt nod of assent. "All right. Purline, bring out the vichyssoise, and be sure to top each serving with a snip of scallions like I showed you. Meanwhile…" He turned to Derrick, his expression grim. "We have got a rabbit to capture."

~8~

Maddie did not find her husband in their room. What she did find was the legal folder open on the bed where she had left it, its contents torn and shredded and scattered over the floor. She picked up the top page, which had been torn in half, her heart in her throat. *Petition for Divorce...*

Suddenly all she could think about was the night Parker was born. Benton had been working late when she called to say she was in labor. She'd gone straight to the hospital while he drove through a rain storm to reach her. He'd had a flat tire, tried to change it, failed, and jogged the last mile and a half to the hospital. He'd arrived just as they were taking her into the delivery room, soaked and streaked with grease, and she hadn't been able to tell whether the wetness on his face was rain or tears. But he'd been there, holding her hand, when Parker made his entrance into the world.

And then she remembered when she'd gotten the job offer in Chicago. She hadn't thought she'd take it. Benton was doing so well, and they'd just started to settle into the Pacific Northwest. But she knew she'd never have an opportunity like this again. Benton had come home that night with a dozen roses and said, "Can't live without you, babe. We're moving."

She pressed a hand over her lips and squeezed her eyes shut against hot tears. *Can't live without you, babe.*

"Damn it," she whispered. *"Damn it."*

She swiped a hand across her dripping nose, blinked hard, and looked down at the crumpled papers on the bed. It wasn't like Benton to lose his temper or show his displeasure in such an obvious way, but could she really blame him? They used to be there for each other. If there was one thing they each had always been able to count on, it was that they would be there for each other.

And now, when Maddie tried to imagine her life without Benton in it, the emptiness was so large it threatened to swallow her whole.

Maddie turned and left the room as she'd found it, closing the door behind her.

Everyone was still gathered in the back garden, taking liberal advantage of their hosts' generosity with the free cocktails before dinner. It took Maddie awhile to make her way through the throng of her in-laws and siblings, returning their embraces and accepting their compliments on what a wonderful choice she had made for the anniversary celebration and what a great idea it was for them all to get together like this. Everyone had some remark to make about the incident with the rabbit, a story which their mother had apparently been exploiting to its fullest. Benton was talking with her father, and Maddie reached the two of them just as dinner was called by one of their rather harried-looking hosts. Her dad hugged her and made some joke about rabbit being on the dinner menu, and they all started toward the dining room together.

Maddie hung back as they reached the French doors, and Benton, reading the anxiety on her face, murmured, "Don't worry, I'm not going to say anything. I know how to play a role."

Maddie said, "I picked up your phone by accident." She handed it to him.

He looked at it in mild surprise, then tucked it into his pocket. "Didn't even miss it."

He gestured her to precede him into the dining room, but Maddie stood still. She smiled absently at her brother-in-law, who moved past her inside. She said, "Dr. Hillsman called about your test results. He wants to see you — us —Monday morning at 9:00."

A shield came over his eyes, and he said with absolutely no expression, "Okay. Thanks. I'll call him back."

"It's the weekend. They're out of the office."

He started to move inside. She caught his arm. "What kind of biopsy did they do?" she demanded, keeping her voice low.

He almost seemed for a moment as though he wouldn't answer, then he said, "Liver."

Maddie felt the blow in the pit of her stomach. She let her hand fall from his arm. Somehow she managed to draw a breath. "So," she said. "That's why you've lost weight. This is serious."

"I was going to talk to you about it," he said, shifting his gaze. "We should make a plan about what to tell the kids. I thought we'd have time to talk on the plane, but you were busy and..." he gave a small shrug. "It didn't seem like the right time. Anyway, best to wait until after I see the doctor Monday."

Maddie another calming breath. "All right," she said, thinking it through quickly. "All right. You were right to be angry. This whole thing about the divorce was stupid and—and ill-timed. You should have said something sooner, but that doesn't matter now. Obviously, you'll move back home full time, and so will I. You'll need someone to take care of you. We'll get through this. Don't worry."

He stared at her, and the expression on his face was not at all what she had expected. "No," he said.

She took an instinctive step back. "What?"

He repeated firmly, "No. I don't want you to move back home. I don't want you to take care of me. I don't want your pity. This is one thing you can't fix, manage or control, Maddie, and I'd appreciate it if for once you didn't try. Now, let's go in." He held out his arm to her. "They're waiting dinner for us."

"Well, I told you boys to expect a little drama," Harmony said, threading her arm through Derrick's as they walked to the reception area. "And aside from the rabbit..."

"Which we still haven't found," Derrick put in glumly.

"Aside from that," reiterated Harmony, "I thought dinner was perfectly lovely. The anniversary couple certainly seemed to enjoy it."

The party had adjourned to the back garden, which was beautifully lit with fairy lights and tiki torches, for after dinner drinks, and to the front parlor, where Paul had provided a fire in the fireplace for those who found the garden too chilly. It was always refreshing to host a family who actually seemed to enjoy one another's company, and the group seemed far from close to running out of things to chat about. This was good news for Paul and Derrick, who still had more than one fire to put out.

"Mrs. Rockwell hardly touched her dinner," Derrick fretted. "I think she was still upset about the incident with the rabbit. Or maybe she was concerned with our sanitation practices." A shadow of alarm crossed his face. "You don't think she'll report us, do you? Our innkeeper's license specifies we're a no-pets-allowed facility. Not to mention our insurance policy."

"Nonsense, darling. Rabbits aren't pets, everyone knows that. They're wild animals. Now, I think the bigger question is what did we decide about the officiant for tomorrow's ceremony?"

Derrick smothered a groan. "I don't think a decision has been made. But," he added quickly, "I do recall Mrs. Rockwell specifically said 'no shaman'."

Harmony's expression fell. "Well, that's rather small-minded of her."

"I suppose. But right now we have to decide what to do about these anniversary gifts we're supposed to surprise our guests-of-honor with. The bride wants to give her husband a week in Palm Springs, and the groom wants to give his wife the trip of a lifetime to Fiji. I left the Fiji tickets on your desk, because you really are genius at clever wrapping and presentation, but now I'm not sure it's even appropriate. Should we tell the couple they're working at cross-purposes? Is it any of our business? Or should we just wrap the gifts as we were told and let them sort it out? I swear, Harmony, I'm starting to think this entire event is cursed."

They both fell silent as they came in sight of the reception desk and saw Benton Rockwell standing there. Derrick came forward quickly. "Mr. Rockwell, good evening. Something I can help you with? More towels? Coffee service in your room?"

He said, "Oh, good. I was just about to text you. I wasn't sure anyone would be at the desk this time of day."

Harmony smiled and went through the half-gate that led to the reception office. "We're always here to help. Would you like to schedule a spa appointment after all? I noticed you weren't in my book."

"No," he said, and looked mildly uncomfortable. "Actually, I was wondering… since the minister was a no-show and his room is sitting empty, and since I assume we paid for it in advance…" He hesitated, as though expecting one of them to finish the sentence, but both Derrick and Harmony looked blank. He went on determinedly, "I was wondering if it would be okay if I took that room for the weekend."

Derrick's eyes flashed with curiosity, but Harmony was an experienced hotelier and didn't even blink. She took the one remaining key from the pegboard behind her and smiled as she handed it to him. "Of course. It's the Peacock room, the one with the turquoise door. It's all set up, but if you need anything just give us a call."

He took the key, mumbled his thanks, and hurried away.

Derrick waited until he was out of sight to murmur, "Well, I guess that explains why his wife was upset at dinner. They must have had a fight."

Harmony said, "Poor things. How awful to quarrel on vacation."

Derrick replied, "I told you this event was cursed."

She held up a cautionary finger. "Not cursed, my dear. Just in a temporary slump. All's well that ends well, you know."

He sighed. "If you say so. Now, what shall we do about the tickets?"

Harmony moved around the papers on her desk with an expression that grew more and more perplexed. "Tickets?" she said. She held up one of the colorful cards with "Guest Pass" embossed across it. "Do you mean this? Shouldn't there be two?"

Derrick surged forward in alarm just as Paul burst through from his own office, his expression indignant, a black and gold ticket held aloft in his hand. The other hand held a pile of shredded black and gold paper. "Do rabbits eat paper?" he demanded.

~10~

Maddie didn't think about it often, but when she did, she knew she was one of the lucky ones. She genuinely liked her brothers and sisters, despite Jackson's tendency to dominate a conversation and Ashley's more-or-less constant whining. They got along. Her parents had given them a loving, supportive environment in which to grow and everyone had thrived. Maddie had tried to do the same for her children, and now she was failing.

That was the first time since her marriage had begun to unravel that she had admitted that. And now, for the first time in her life, she was forced to admit something else: she didn't know what to do.

While her sisters, all giggles and outrageous stories, took a couple of bottles of wine into one of their rooms for a trying-on-the-dresses party and the men—most of them anyway— took a very expensive bottle of brandy that Jackson had given their dad into the parlor to enjoy in front of the fire, Maddie went in search of her husband. She didn't find him, and she thought he must have gone back to their room. She started to go there herself, but she spotted her mother sitting in the swing on the front porch. Claire smiled when she saw Maddie and beckoned her over.

"I was just looking for Benton," Maddie said.

"Come sit for a moment," Claire said, patting the place on the swing beside her. "What's going on with you two, anyway? You didn't say two words between you at dinner, and you let that beautiful trout go to waste."

Maddie, hesitated, and then sat. With absolutely no intention of saying it, she heard her voice replying, "Benton and I have been separated for four months." She was amazed at how easily the confession came out, after all the time she had spent dreading it. "He kissed a woman at the office Christmas party. Stupid. It was a one time thing, not worth wrecking a marriage over, but it was… wrong. One minute I had the perfect marriage and the next there was this big stain on my perfect life that I couldn't get out, and it was his fault. I didn't have a choice, did I? When a person cheats on you the marriage is over. The trust is broken. That's just the way it is." She took a breath. "I should have told you before, but I don't know. I think I didn't know how. Everyone counts on me to be in charge, to get things right, and I just didn't know how to admit that I'd screwed up my marriage. And now… I think I've made an even bigger mistake. I just served Benton with divorce papers. And a divorce is the last thing I want."

Maddie didn't know whether her mother's silence was shocked, sympathetic, or disapproving. She found, to her great surprise, that it didn't matter. If she had told the truth sooner—to herself, her family, to Benton—so much pain could have been avoided. Even now, saying the words out loud felt like an enormous burden had been lifted from her shoulders.

After a long time, Claire reached over and gently squeezed her daughter's hand. "The curse of being the oldest child," she said, "is constantly trying to meet everyone else's expectations. It's even worse when what everyone expects is for you to be perfect. I know. I was the oldest child. And, if you recall, your grandpa—sweet old bear that he was—could be a little stern. Perfection was not an option for him; it was a requirement. So, when he found out his oldest child was pregnant before she even finished college…"

Maddie sat up straight, staring at her mother. "What?"

Claire just smiled. "That's right. That beautiful country-club wedding fifty years ago was thrown together in less than two weeks, something I believe they called a shotgun wedding back then, and you, my darling, were the guest of honor. That's the real reason I look so plump in the photographs—I was almost five months pregnant with you. Before that, Henry and I had no intention of getting married. We'd only been dating a couple of months, and we barely knew each other, now that I look back on it. But times were different back then, and Henry was a Naval officer, and it was what you did. And, of course, there was my dad."

Maddie shook her head slowly, regarding her mother in an entirely new light. "But…all this time… how could I not have known?"

"Well," admitted Claire, "I'm afraid I changed the date on your birth certificate. Or, rather, my mother did. You were actually born August 18, not February 18."

Maddie gasped. "You tampered with an official document?"

Claire gave a helpless shrug. "I'm really sorry, sweetheart, but I'm afraid you're actually six months older than you think. Like I said, it was a different time."

Maddie sank back heavily against the plush pillows of the swing, trying to digest this.

"The point I wanted to make," Claire said, "is that trying to live a perfect life never, ever works out. Especially when you're trying to live up to somebody's else's idea of perfection."

Maddie blew out a long breath of disbelief. "So, I was conceived out of wedlock. Not so perfect after all. Jackson is going to have a field day with this."

Claire chuckled softly. "He will, won't he? And who knows? Maybe you can ease up on yourself a little, too."

"Yeah," murmured Maddie. "Maybe."

Claire said earnestly, "Don't misunderstand me, honey. Henry and I have had a wonderful life, and you children were the highlight of it. We've always been terribly fond of each other—although I'm not at all sure how long that fondness would have lasted if he hadn't spent most of his life on an aircraft carrier and I hadn't spent most of mine in Norfolk. We're still each other's best friend, make no mistake. But it was only after he retired, and all you children were off living your own lives, that we came to realize how very little we actually had in common."

She paused for a moment, organizing her thoughts. "Before we knew you'd planned this anniversary party," she went on, "and it really is lovely, darling, and so thoughtful… but last year, before all of this came up, your father and I had already decided to separate. We didn't want to spoil the party by telling you kids."

Maddie stared at her mother. "Didn't want to…" Her voice was choked. "But… but.. everything is okay now, right? You worked it out?"

Claire's face was serene in the reflected lamplight from the house. "Oh, yes. We're happier than we've ever been."

And just as Maddie's shoulders began to sag with relief, Claire went on, "Your father moved into the guest house last spring, completely remodeled it, even put in a deck with a hot tub. He has his life and I have mine. He's even seeing someone, off and on, a perfectly lovely woman. A CPA. And don't look so shocked. I've had a fling or two myself. The point is, we're both happy. We're living the lives we were meant to live. We hardly ever see each other, but when we do it's because we want to, and we enjoy each other's company. Like this weekend. It was a wonderful idea, but really, one weekend is just about as long as we can stand each other. That why, for the Palm Springs trip, I booked myself a separate suite."

And at her daughter's horrified look, she chuckled softly. "Oh, sweetheart, fifty years is a long time. I'm not at all sure nature ever intended two people to live together that long, even under the best of circumstances. Think about it. It's only been in the past couple of hundred years that people have even *lived* past fifty. It's unnatural."

Maddie managed, "Are you going to get a divorce?"

Claire laughed lightly. "Heavens, no. After fifty years, our lives are far too complex for that. We both love our beautiful house on the river, and we like having a place for the grandchildren to come visit. How could we ever untangle our finances? Besides, we've grown used to each other, and at our age, it's nice to know someone else is around, you know? Someone you can count on."

Maddie said, "But... the commitment ceremony! The vows renewal! The recreation of the wedding photograph... why did you ever agree to all of that?"

Claire gave a small shrug, and her tone was a little wry. "Well, honey, when the idea of the anniversary get-together first came up, we had no idea it would be this elaborate. We actually thought this weekend would be the perfect time to tell you children about our new living arrangements. Believe me, I would have stopped the ceremony if I could have. But you did all this planning, ordered the dresses, made the arrangements... and by the time I saw what you had in mind, it was too late. You would have lost all the money you put into this, and everyone would have been so disappointed. Henry and I decided we could go along with the charade for one weekend. After all, just because our lives have changed doesn't mean we're not still committed to our family, so the ceremony isn't really a lie, now is it?" She smiled. "I have to say though, I am a little relieved that the minister couldn't make it."

The smile faded, and her fingers tightened round Maddie's. "Darling, all I want to tell you is not to let what other people expect of you define who you are. Once you were crazy enough about Benton to defy every convention and elope to Las Vegas with him, even though you'd been dreaming about a big wedding all your life. You moved across the country to make him happy, and then he moved back across the country for you. There was a time in your life when you figured things out together, when you made decisions with your heart and not with your head."

Maddie was silent for a long time, breathing slowly, trying to keep the tears from filling up her throat. She said at last, brokenly, "I don't know what to do."

"Oh, sweetheart." Claire put an arm around her daughter's shoulders and hugged her fiercely. "I think you do. You're just afraid to try. You have to do what's right for your life, and your marriage, the same way I did." She leaned back and smiled at Maddie in the dim light. "Just don't take fifty years to find out what the right thing is, okay?"

~11~

Maddie found Benton in their room. His duffle was open on the bench at the foot of the bed, and he turned when she opened the door, pieces of the shredded divorce papers in his hand. "So," he said. His expression was uncertain, like the one a man might have who was looking at a winning lottery ticket: wanting to believe it, but afraid to. "You were serious?"

Maddie came forward quickly. "Benton, listen. I never wanted to end our marriage, I just wanted to punish you. For hurting me, for making me feel I wasn't enough, for—"

"You were always enough," he interrupted quickly.

She shook her head briefly. "I put our marriage on automatic pilot. I stopped working at it. But it wasn't because I didn't care, it was because I could. Because it was the one sure and easy thing I could count on in my life. And now, when I think of life without you…"

"Wait." He held up a hand for silence. His face was taut, and so was his voice. "If you're saying this because I'm sick, because you think I might be dying, don't. I told you before, I don't want your pity and that's certainly nothing to build a marriage on. Besides…" He drew a breath. "I'm fine."

While she stared at him, not understanding, he went on, "I called Jim Hillsman after dinner. For God's sake, we've played golf together for fifteen years, do you really think he'd let me go a whole weekend wondering? It's not cancer. His girl was supposed to tell me that. It's a small tumor, there may be a surgery, and that's what he wanted to talk to us—to me—about Monday." He drew a long slow breath and let it out. "I'm fine."

Maddie stumbled into his arms. "Oh my God, oh my God," she whispered. She was shaking. "I'm so glad, Benton. I'm so glad. I don't want to lose you."

He held her shoulders and looked down at her, his expression somber. "Really? I know I hurt you, honey, and you have every right to hate me. I screwed up. I was stupid. I know sorry isn't enough and I've spent every hour of the past four months beating myself up about it. I hurt you and that's the last thing I ever wanted to do. But..." he drew a breath and finished quietly, "I'm not willing to go back to the way things were, Maddie."

"Me either," she said hoarsely. She searched his eyes, hungry for some sign that he believed her. "It wasn't until... until I thought I might really lose you forever that I realized how much I need you in my life. How much I need our partnership, how much better I am with you than without you. I don't want to be in charge of everything anymore. It's exhausting. Perfection is exhausting. I just want..." There was a catch in her voice, but she smiled through it. "I just want the man who picked plastic flowers for my wedding bouquet. Who held my hand when our babies were born. Who put a bikini top and a feather boa on our snowman, and who knows the answer to every stupid trivia question ever written. I want to be with you, Benton. I'll do whatever it takes to make you believe that."

He smiled faintly and glanced around at the shredded papers strewn from the floor to the bed. "I think you made that pretty clear when you tore up the divorce papers. I have to say, I didn't expect that. "

She followed his gaze in confusion. "But...I didn't do that. I thought you did."

His brows drew together. "I signed the papers before dinner. I just came back to get my things. I was going to move to the empty room for the night. But when I saw this..." Again, he gestured to the torn and crumpled document scattered across the room, and he fell silent. After a moment, he smiled. "Well," he said. "It looks like someone wants us to give it another shot."

"I'm onboard with that," she said softly, searching his face. "What about you?"

For a moment he didn't speak, and then he drew her slowly into his arms. "Yeah," he said. "Me too."

~12~

Forty-five minutes before the ceremony, the Hummingbird House was abuzz. The ladies were zipping themselves into their finery, the men were laughing at their peach and lilac cummerbunds and cursing the bow ties. The florist delivered bouquets and set up the big urns of peach and cream roses on either side of the garden arch. The luncheon tables were dressed in white lace tablecloths and Haviland china, with a tasteful arrangement of one peach and one cream rose under a glass dome in the center of each. The harpist warmed up from her shaded corner of the big porch while the photographer set up her equipment. The three-tier wedding cake, topped with an exquisitely crafted, hand-painted pair of confectioner's turtledoves, was prominently displayed on a tall, satin-covered table. And in the butler's pantry, one long-eared, big-eyed bunny rabbit was safely ensconced in his cage, munching on a carrot.

Paul and Derrick stood very still, hardly daring to believe it. Derrick demanded, "Purline, how did you do it?" He kept his voice low, as though afraid anything above a whisper would undo whatever magic had finally captured the creature.

"Oh, please." Purline shoved her way between them and reached for a glass platter on the back shelf. "While you two was running around like a couple of chickens with your heads cut off…"

"I really wish you wouldn't use that phrase," Paul said with a stifled groan. "Such unfortunate imagery."

"Turning over mattresses, pulling out drawers," she went on, ignoring him, "I just propped open the cage door with a stick and put a carrot inside. After everything finally quieted down last night, Mr. Earnest there hopped on in to have himself a snack, knocked over the stick, the door closed and locked him in. Learned that in Girl Scouts."

She strode past them with the platter in hand, her pony tail swinging in a particularly smug way. Paul, after one more dark look at the rabbit in the cage, said, "Nevertheless, a padlock on that door wouldn't hurt."

"No need," she replied. "My mama is bringing little Jacob over to collect him in a minute. Now, do you want these chicken thingies served with the soup or after it?"

"After!" Derrick and Paul said at once, both of them hurrying forward.

Purline shooed them away, using the platter like a fan. "Get on out of my kitchen then, both of you! You want this thing to go off on time, don't you? Then go on and find something else to do."

Paul looked at Derrick. Derrick tilted his head to him in sorrowful assent.

"I guess we can't put it off any longer," Paul said.

"We've done our best," agreed Derrick. "We have to tell her."

Paul squared his shoulders. "Then let's go."

~13~

"Oh my God," said Maddie. She came in from the bathroom with the peach dress completely open in the back, clutching it to her bosom with one hand. There was panic in her eyes. "The dressmaker made a mistake! This dress is three sizes too small! I should have double-checked. I should have had it sent to my house so I could try it on. I should have..."

Benton turned from the mirror, resplendent in lilac cummerbund and mangled bow tie, and spread out his hands. "You think you've got problems," he said.

Maddie stared at him for a moment, then burst into laughter. She walked into his embrace. "I think you look gorgeous," she said.

"And I think you're amazing," he said, and kissed her.

They parted reluctantly at the sound of a knock on the door. "Maddie, honey," Claire called from outside the door. "Is this a bad time?"

Maddie gave her husband an apologetic look and went to answer the door. "Mom, I'm so sorry," she began. "There seems to be a problem with..."

She broke off and her mother, wearing a white gown that was easily three sizes too big, finished for her, "The dress."

Maddie pressed her fingers to her lips. "Oh, my goodness," she said. "Oh, no. Mom, I swear, I gave the seamstress your measurements, I checked with her three times..."

Claire shrugged helplessly. "I guess she made a mistake." She looked at Benton, and she smiled. "My, don't you look nice, though?" She added innocently, "Did you two have a good evening?"

Benton understood the weight of the question and answered it with a tender, lingering look at his wife. "Perfect," he said. And then he looked back at Claire. "Ladies, if you don't mind, I may have an idea…"

~14~

Paul and Derrick were headed to the guest rooms when they stopped short. Maddie Rockwell was coming down the hall toward them, looking radiant in a perfectly fitted white wedding gown. The skirt was so wide it practically brushed the walls on either side of the corridor, and the gossamer veil trailed two feet behind her. Her mother and three sisters, all in peach gowns with green sashes, were huddled at the other end of the hall, conferring busily.

"Oh, good!" Maddie exclaimed, extending her gloved hands to them. "I was just coming to look for you. There's been a slight change of plans."

"So it would appear." Paul prided himself on his sangfroid, but he couldn't prevent a blink of surprise before his genial smile was back in place.

"Apparently, the seamstress misunderstood my instructions," Maddie explained, "and mixed up my measurements with my mother's. As it turns out…" She opened one palm in a gesture of shy surrender. "My mother wasn't all that interested in recreating her wedding day, and since I never actually had a real wedding, she insisted that we switch places."

"You look lovely, Mrs. Rockwell," Paul said sincerely. "We just wanted to let you know that everything is on schedule and in place. There was just one thing we thought we should mention…"

"A tiny hiccup, at best," Derrick assured her.

"The problem is that it was supposed to be a surprise," Paul added, "so we weren't entirely sure what to do…"

"It really was a lovely gesture, and we did everything we could to bring it to fruition," Derrick went on earnestly. "Two gestures, really. Two lovely gestures. Unfortunately…"

Maddie looked from one to the other of them in confusion, and Paul concluded frankly. "The thing is, Mrs. Rockwell, your parents each entrusted us with a gift for the other, a honeymoon surprise, if you will. That was a dilemma in itself, since the honeymoon destinations were to two different places, and at the same time."

Maddie's brow knitted with puzzlement. "I don't think I follow."

"Your father," explained Derrick, "gifted his wife with two tickets to her dream destination—Fiji."

"And your mother," added Paul, "gave your father the honeymoon he had always wanted at a golf resort in Palm Springs. They each had the most beautiful custom tickets printed up. We were entrusted with wrapping the gifts and presenting the surprises at luncheon."

Maddie started to laugh softly. Paul and Derrick exchanged an uneasy glance.

"The problem," Paul went on, "is that, through an unfortunate accident—"

"Not of our making," Derrick was quick to point out.

Paul gave a brisk nod of assent and went on, "One ticket from each set was destroyed before we could wrap them. We tried to replicate them on our computer, but, as I said—custom. So sadly, all we have to present to your mother for her honeymoon surprise is one ticket to Fiji. And for your father, one ticket to Palm Springs. We couldn't feel worse about it, honestly."

Maddie's eyes were still bright with amusement, "Actually gentlemen, there's no need to apologize. Just wrap up what you have. I have a feeling this is going to be the best vacation either of them ever had."

Paul and Derrick shared a confused look, and then an uncertain smile. "Well," said Derrick. "As long as you're happy..."

Maddie said sincerely, "Honestly, I couldn't be happier. There was just one other thing. I know I made a big fuss about having an ordained minister for the ceremony, but with the change in the cast of characters, it actually doesn't matter after all." She smiled. "In fact, Benton and I would frankly prefer a layman. Or lay woman. So, if it's not too terribly much trouble..."

Paul drew back his shoulders, beaming. "Not in the slightest," he declared. "In fact, I do believe I have the perfect solution in mind."

~15~

Harmony, in a peach silk caftan and a turban printed with lavender hydrangeas, stood between Paul and Derrick, watching benevolently as the photographer lined up the wedding party for the photograph. "There now, boys," she said, slipping an arm through each of theirs. "Didn't I tell you everything would turn out? A tiny bit of drama, but Mrs. Rockwell got to have the wedding of her dreams, Mrs. Swenson gets the honeymoon of her dreams…"

"Without Mr. Swenson," Derrick pointed out a little uneasily.

"But he also gets the honeymoon of his dreams," Harmony went on, "without Mrs. Swenson."

"Which I still think is bizarre," Derrick looked offended. "The two of them are the sweetest couple I've ever met, and they obviously care enough about each other to arrange these expensive trips neither one of them wanted to take just in order to make the other one happy. But it turns out they're not even a *couple*?"

"I have to agree," Paul said, frowning. "the entire situation is just a little off."

Harmony gave each of them a look of mild reproof. "There are many types of relationships," she pointed out, "as the two of you should very well know. And love can be expressed in a myriad of ways. Just because they don't want to live in each other's pockets doesn't mean they can't still be devoted. And I would say that after fifty years, one deserves a little adventure, wouldn't you?"

Both men looked unwillingly chastised. "I suppose you're right, Harmony," Derrick said. "It just seems to me everything would have gone so much more smoothly if they'd all be honest with each other from the beginning."

"But look how happy the Rockwells are now," Harmony said, smiling in their direction. "And you, my dear..." She glanced at Paul. "Performed a perfectly lovely renewal ceremony."

Paul adjusted the lapel of his dove gray suit, looking pleased with himself. "It was quite nice, wasn't it?" he agreed, and added generously, "Of course, your blessing of the marriage was really the finishing touch."

"So, you see," Harmony said happily, "everyone got exactly what they needed. And look." She gestured at the carefully posed group before the garden arch—the bride in white, the bridesmaids in peach, the gentlemen in their bow ties and cummerbunds. The photographer folded his fingers one by one, counting down—three, two, one—and snapped the photograph. "The perfect picture!"

And, except for the small brown bunny standing unnoticed on the bride's trailing veil, it was.

~*~

Also in this series:

The Hummingbird House
Christmas at the Hummingbird House

And don't miss

The Ladybug Farm series
Before The Hummingbird House

A Year on Ladybug Farm
At Home on Ladybug Farm
Love Letters from Ladybug Farm
Christmas on Ladybug Farm
Recipes from Ladybug Farm
Vintage Ladybug Farm
A Wedding on Ladybug Farm

~*~

Also by this Author

The Raine Stockton Dog Mystery Series Books in Order

SMOKY MOUNTAIN TRACKS
A child has been kidnapped and abandoned in the mountain wilderness. Her only hope is Raine Stockton and her young, untried tracking dog Cisco...
RAPID FIRE

Raine and Cisco are brought in by the FBI to track a terrorist ...a terrorist who just happens to be Raine's old boyfriend.

GUN SHY

Raine rescues a traumatized service dog, and soon begins to suspect he is the only witness to a murder.

BONE YARD

Cisco digs up human remains in Raine's back yard, and mayhem ensues. Could this be evidence of a serial killer, a long-unsolved mass murder, or something even more sinister... and closer to home?

SILENT NIGHT

It's Christmastime in Hansonville, N.C., and Raine and Cisco are on the trail of a missing teenager. But when a newborn is abandoned in the manger of the town's living nativity and Raine walks in on what appears to be the scene of a murder, the holidays take a very dark turn for everyone concerned.

THE DEAD SEASON

Raine and Cisco accept a job leading troubled teenagers on a winter wilderness hike, and soon find themselves trapped on a mountainside... with a killer.

ALL THAT GLITTERS: A Raine and Cisco Christmas short story

In this holiday short story, learn how Raine and Cisco first met and solved their debut mystery together.

HIGH IN TRIAL

A weekend competition turns deadly when Raine and Cisco travel to South Carolina for some R&R, unaware that a twenty year old mystery is unfolding back home that will have devastating consequences for both Raine and the people she loves.

DOUBLE DOG DARE

Raine and Cisco travel to the Caribbean for a well-deserved vacation, but even in paradise trouble finds them.

HOME OF THE BRAVE

There's a new dog in town, and Raine and Cisco find themselves unexpectedly upstaged by a flashy K-9 addition to the sheriff's department. But when things go terribly wrong at a mountain camp for kids and dogs over the Fourth of July weekend, Raine and Cisco need all the help they can get to save themselves, and those they love.

DOG DAYS

Raine takes in a lost English Cream Golden Retriever, and the search for her owner leads Raine and Cisco into the hands of a killer. Readers will enjoy a treasure hunt for the titles of all ten of the Raine Stockton Dog Mysteries hidden in this special tenth anniversary release!

LAND OF THE FREE

On a routine search and rescue mission Raine Stockton and her golden retriever Cisco stumble onto something they were never meant to find, and are plunged into a nightmare of murder, corruption and intrigue as figures from her past re-emerge to threaten everything Raine holds dear.

DEADFALL

Hollywood comes to Hanover County, and Raine and Cisco get caught up in the drama when a series of mishaps on the set lead to murder.

THE DEVIL'S DEAL

Raine takes temporary custody of what may well be the most valuable dog in the world, but when lives are at stake she is forced to make an unthinkable choice.

MURDER CREEK

Raine and Cisco rescue a dog who is locked in a hot car in a remote Smoky Mountain park... and subsequently discover the owner of that car drowned in the creek only a few dozen yards away. Was it an accident, or was it murder?

Don't miss the powerful new Dogleg Island Mystery Series

FLASH

Almost two years ago the sleepy little community of Dogleg Island was the scene of one of the most brutal crimes in Florida history. The only eye witnesses were a border collie puppy and a police officer. Since that time Flash has grown from a puppy into a vital part of the Dogleg Island Police Department, and has lived happily with the two people who rescued him on that horrible night: Deputy Sheriff Ryan Grady and Police Chief Aggie Malone.

Now the trial of the century is about to begin. The defendant, accused of slaughtering his parents in their beach home, maintains his innocence. Aggie and Ryan, the top witnesses for the prosecution, are convinced he is lying. But only Flash knows the truth.

And with another murder to solve, a tangle of conflicting evidence to sort out, and a brutal storm on the way, the truth may come too late... for all of them.

THE SOUND OF RUNNING HORSES
Dogleg Island Mystery #2

A family outing takes a dark turn when Flash, Aggie and Grady discover a body on deserted Wild Horse Island, and the evidence appears to point to someone they know — and trust.

FLASH OF BRILLIANCE
Dogleg Island Mystery #3

Aggie, Flash and Grady look forward to their first Christmas as a family until a homicide hit-and-run exposes a crime syndicate, and dark shadows from the past return to haunt their future.

PIECES OF EIGHT
A deadly explosion at an archeological dig on Dogleg Island plunges police chief Aggie Malone and her canine partner Flash into a dark mystery from the past, while on the other side of the bridge, Deputy Sheriff Ryan Grady, stumbles onto the site of a mass murder. As the investigation unfolds, Aggie and Grady see that two two cases are related, but only Flash knows how…and by whom.

***More** spine-chilling suspense by Donna Ball*

NIGHT FLIGHT
She's an innocent woman who knows too much. Now she's fleeing through the night without a weapon and without a phone, and her only hope for survival is a cop who's willing to risk his badge—and his life—to save her.

SHATTERED
A missing child, a desperate call for help in the middle of the night… is this a cruel hoax, or the work of a maniacal serial killer who is poised to strike again?

EXPOSURE
Everyone has secrets, but when talk show host Jessamine Cray's stalker begins to use her past to terrorize her, no one is safe … not her family, her friends, her coworkers, and especially not Jess herself.

RENEGADE by Donna Boyd
Enter a world of dark mystery and intense passion, where human destiny is controlled by a species of powerful, exotic creatures. Once they ruled the Tundra, now they rule Wall Street. Once they fought with teeth and claws, now they fight with wealth and power. And only one man can stop them… if he dares.

About the Author

Donna Ball is the author of over a hundred novels under several different pseudonyms in a variety of genres that include romance, mystery, suspense, paranormal, western adventure, historical and women's fiction. Recent popular series include the Ladybug Farm series, The Hummingbird House series, The Dogleg Island Mystery series, and the Raine Stockton Dog Mystery series. She lives in a restored Victorian Barn in the heart of the Blue Ridge Mountains with a variety of four-footed companions. You can contact her at

www.donnaball.net.

Made in the USA
Coppell, TX
11 September 2020